LOVE SONGS OF THE REVOLUTION

A NOVEL

BRONWYN MAULDIN

CHICAGO CENTER FOR LITERATURE AND PHOTOGRAPHY
2014

Printed and distributed by the Chicago Center for
Literature and Photography. *First paperback edition, first
printing: May 2014.*

Cover: Ryan W. Bradley

ISBN: 978-1-939987-21-1

Photo credits: Extra No. 2: "Vilniaus Panorama," by
Wikimedia member TiredTime. Extra No. 5: "Doug
Liman at the Cannes Film Festival, 2010," by Wikimedia
member BearWithClaws. Extra No. 7: "Untitled,"
by Ahmet Demirel. All images released to the public
domain voluntarily by their owners, and found at
Wikimedia.org.

This collection is also available in a variety of electronic
formats, including EPUB for mobile devices, MOBI for
Kindles, and PDFs for both American and European
laserprinters, as well as a special deluxe handmade
hardback edition. Find them all, plus a plethora of
supplemental information such as interviews, videos and
reviews, at:

cclapcenter.com/lovesongs

To Mom and Dad
for teaching me to explore

CAST OF CHARACTERS

Martynas Kudirka: Lithuanian painter and loyal member of the Communist Party

Natalie Milosz: Martynas's wife

Žemyna: Martynas's lover

Gintaras Degutis: Natalie's student

Indre Bučienė: Natalie's lover

Jonas Rimša: Chief Inspector in the Vilnius police

Leonas Songaila: Man from the Ministry of Internal Affairs

Romas Sakadolskis: Presenter on Voice of America broadcasts into Lithuania

Vanda Sadunaitė: Martynas and Natalie's neighbor across the hall

Adolfas: Žemyna's boss

Antanas: Member of the Lithuanian independence movement

Kurt Parable: American with ties to the Lithuanian independence movement

Pablo: Young tough

Justas: Member of the Lithuanian independence movement

Stasys: Member of the Lithuanian independence movement

Sąjūdis: Lithuanian independence movement

FROM VILNIUS:
MINSK: 115 MILES
WARSAW: 283 MILES
KIEV: 450 MILES
STOCKHOLM: 490 MILES
MOSCOW: 586 MILES
BERLIN: 634 MILES
COPENHAGEN: 901 MILES

PART 1

ONE ➤

AH, MY BELOVED VILNIUS, HOW I MISS YOU.
You who speak only English cannot hear the beauty of that name. You hear words like "villain" and "vile." Perhaps you hear "village," the word for a backward, bygone place that no longer exists in America.

Vilnius was the city of my childhood, my youth, and my manhood. Everything that mattered in my life happened in Vilnius. Since I left Vilnius, nothing that has happened in my life has mattered to anyone, least of all me. I was born in Vilnius. There I was wrapped in a mother's love. I had my eleven years of compulsory schooling and went to university to study art. I painted my first picture in Vilnius, of a girl so beautiful I could scarcely bear to look at her as I applied paint to canvas. The first time I made love to a woman we lay beneath that painting, in the back bedroom of my mother's small apartment in Vilnius. I married in Vilnius. And it was in Vilnius that I found my beautiful wife dead on the kitchen floor with a knife in her back.

I warn you now, my fellow Americans—yes, I am a citizen by choice now in your country—you will be disappointed by this story. You measure the quality of literature by the complexity of its plot twists. Unpredictability and "originality" are valued above all else. You insist on a happy ending, or at least a glimpse of a silver lining behind every cloud. You want to know that no animals were harmed in the making of this story. I can promise you none of this.

The story I am going to tell is true; therefore it will not please you. It is direct and straightforward. The dead remain dead, and the guilty go unpunished. The sepia-tinted dream you might wish it to be turns out to be a dull, faded reality. When you close this book, you will frown and use words like "unresolved." You will come to conclusions, and ask why no one took the actions that are plainly obvious to you.

That is because you are Americans, and you believe there is a solution to every problem. That every grief concludes in closure, or that it should. That hard work pays off, and cream always rises to the top. That every crime can be solved in an hour, minus eighteen minutes for commercial breaks. That satisfaction is guaranteed. You are fools to expect anything but heartache and disappointment. It is your expectations that make you weak.

I have wept every day since I escaped from Vilnius. They began as tears of grief for what I had lost. They became tears of rage for unfulfilled promises. Then tears of frustration and impotence, for awakening each morning to realize I must live another day among these amnesiac people.

Today, I weep for being alive when I should be long dead. My seventieth birthday has come and gone. Not so old, you say? Not by your American standards, perhaps. But I have now been almost thirty years away from the country that gave me my identity. If forgetting is the quintessential American pathology, then nostalgia is mine.

If there were a god, he would have made sure the efficient killer that took so many people from me did not leave me to suffer my own survival. He could have made sure the killer's knife took me on the streets of Vilnius that day while my fellow Lithuanians were singing their hearts out for freedom and democracy.

Once I feared the KGB and its Lithuanian sycophants, wheels that turned the relentless machinery of the state. Today I have been reduced to a time and place where my greatest fear is that when I die I will be buried in this dry, dusty city on the edge of this abysmal country. To be buried here is to be forgotten. If a coyote shits on my grave, its feces will dry up and blow away to become part of the haze and pollution that blankets this city, rather than nourishing the growth of another generation of plants.

It is as bad to die in Los Angeles as it is to live here. My will states I should be taken home to Vilnius, but who is here to carry out my wishes? I have no children, no relations near or distant. For that matter, no friends.

You Americans cannot understand what Vilnius means to Lithuanians. For us, the name carries with it the same sophistication and grandeur you mean when you say "New York" or "San Francisco." But your cities have no history. When you say "the history of Chicago" you reach back only a few years and try to mold a transcendent mythology from the Haymarket Riots and Al Capone.

When we say Vilnius, we look back seven centuries to Grand Duke Gediminas whose dream of a wolf made of iron, howling on a hill, was the founding of our city. We speak of a proud pagan people who were the last in Europe to fall to the Christian onslaught. We mean the strength of a culture to survive centuries of occupation by our hated half-brothers, the Poles, who called our city "Wilno" when it was theirs. The countless years of interference by the humorless Germans, who called it "Wilna." The years in the vise grip of the overweening Russians who called our city "Vilna."

What I mean when I say "Vilnius" is the strength of a people to be the first to vote to leave the Soviet Union in 1991, and the persistence to make that vote mean something.

You Americans fault the Soviets for the way they managed their economy and took on client states like greedy jackals. You saw evil in everything they did, while we saw those same actions in shades of gray. They tried to bury our language, yes, but they also freed us from the yoke of a god that would have us live in perpetual apology as you do for the sins of a man and woman who did nothing more than eat an apple in their own private garden.

Mark my words, your invasion of Afghanistan will end as sorrowfully as theirs did, and you will learn as few lessons from it as they. Your need for expansion and control makes you as stupid as the Russians. Your empire will fall one day, and it will rise again, only to fall once more. Meanwhile, Lithuanians will sit at their cafes in Vilnius and drink their *gira*, paint their pictures, make love to their wives and girlfriends, and forget you ever existed.

But who am I to lecture you?

At one time I was Martynas Kudirka, Lithuanian painter and loyal member of the Lithuanian Communist Party. Today I am simply a man. A man, I know only because I still piss standing up.

In Lithuania I was an artist. Not a particularly good one, but a successful one. I was not political. You who were brought up on American Cold War fables will find this surprising, though not without some cause. Most of the great and good artists I knew—Eastern or Western, Baltic or Russian—opposed their governments to one degree or another. I, on the other hand, was a second-rate talent. When mimicking the works of others, my hand was supple. When charged with responsibility for my own style, my wrists and knuckles froze like those of an arthritic old bachelor. I expect this memoir will show me to be much the same in the literary arts. I was unoriginal because I believed all that could be said, had been said. I had nothing to add. I was easy-going and generous, and loved the company of my friends as much as they loved mine, so my fellow art students in the university never mocked my work. They simply had nothing to say about it. On canvases large and small I copied the Soviet Russian greats, as they were taught to us: Russov, Buchkin, Veselova and Semionov. I might put the face of this friend or that lover into the composition, but everything I produced was imitative and unoriginal. And I didn't care.

I was at first surprised when, upon graduation from university, I was selected by the Lithuanian Communist Party's Section for Propaganda and Agitation as an official painter for the state and given a teaching position at the Vilnius Pedagogical Institute. So many of my far more talented peers were passed over. But I wasn't a fool. I understood why they'd chosen me and it didn't stop me from accepting. I simply was grateful for the chance to make a living as a painter. I was as compliant as they expected and joined the party as a matter of course. Even the lowliest party members could get access to fresh meat and sparkling Gewrorgian wines when others went without.

My work was known throughout Lithuania, even if no one knew my name. The Section for Propaganda and Agitation gave my style a title, "Lithuanian Soviet Realism," which sounds as derivative as it was. But I lived a good life. I met beautiful women, wooed them, took them to bed. One of them, I convinced to marry me.

Her name was Natalie Milosz, a Lithuanian girl of Polish descent who had bright, wide-open brown eyes that bulged a little, as if she were impatient to see everything. She was a scientist, after all, and what sets scientists apart from the rest of us is their insatiable curiosity. When I met Natalie she worked in a laboratory at Vilnius

University where she taught radiophysics. Her thinking in her field was far more original than mine was in my field. Despite this, she was as successful in her career as I was, and she soon advanced to a good position.

We were given a large one-bedroom Khrushchev apartment on Erfurto Street in the heart of the Lazdynai District in Vilnius. Large by our standards in that day and time. You Americans with your hands on hips and elbows jutting out akimbo, your sectional sofas and fifty-inch television screens, you would find it cramped and unlivable. It fit our needs, if not well, then adequately.

I had moved my mother into a neighboring apartment in 1978, but she passed away the following year. My father had died of a fever in 1952. Natalie was from a small Polish village. She took the train to visit her mother once a month.

During the week, I painted in my studio and taught at the Pedagogical Institute while Natalie solved radiophysics puzzles in her lab with her own students. We spent the weekends with friends or family. Each of us had little affairs from time to time, but nothing so serious that it threatened our domestic comfort.

It was a pleasant, easy life. We didn't have all the things you Americans seem to find indispensable in your petit bourgeois lives: dishwashers, Diet Cokes, microwave dinners, elevators, cable television. What we had was stronger: friends and family, good food, and work that gave us a deep, abiding personal satisfaction. Natalie eventually became a party member, and we had a few more of the things that make life a little easier.

Then came the summer of 1989.

If you were Lithuanian, or from any of the Baltic countries, the mere mention of this date would cause every nerve in your body to tingle. Images from that year would flood your mind, whether you were on the streets of Vilnius or of Washington, DC, that year.

You would begin to hum the songs of those heady, fateful days, our traditional folk songs, the *Tautiška giesme* or perhaps *Ilgiausiu metu.* Even people such as me who kept ourselves out of politics heard those songs and found ourselves singing along quite accidentally. The music was all around us, floating on the air waves, calling out to us in our sleep.

Do you even know the names of the Baltic countries, my American reader? I'll give you a hint. There are only three. One of them is Lithuania.

If you are Lithuanian, you will read my story one way. If you are not, you will read it very differently. Read this story as your passport demands: a love story, a murder mystery, a story of political intrigue. Perhaps by the final page, those stories will converge.

One otherwise unremarkable afternoon in late August of 1989 I was having lunch with a few artists I knew. A sculptor was visiting from Krakow, and we were on our better behavior for him. We Lithuanians have a love-hate relationship with our neighbors the Poles, but he was an artist like us, so we gave him the benefit of the doubt. He didn't give off the hauteur we'd come to expect from his countrymen, and we'd had a few bottles of beer with our sausages, which gave the afternoon a cheerful edge.

I'd been working in the studio that morning, and was on the verge of finishing a painting of young girls working at an oil refinery in Mažeikiai I'd visited recently. I'd actually seen many men and only one middle-aged woman working there, but the authorities wanted to promote the image of women working in the energy sector. I was telling my friends that in the painting I'd modeled all the girls as variations of my current lover, a Vilnius baker by the name of Žemyna. In exchange, they'd poked friendly fun of my so-called

7

"Lithuanian Soviet Realist" style. The conversation shifted when our Polish sculptor lowered his voice and began talking politics. Free elections for parliament had been held in Poland earlier in the summer, which Solidarity had won handily. Lech Wałęsa's name was on every tongue. My fellow artists leaned forward and returned the favor talking about the latest from Sąjūdis, our own independence movement that had grown up in the wake of Gorbachev's new policies of *perestroika, glasnost* and *khozraschet*. They'd been giving Moscow and the local Lithuanian Communist Party no end of trouble with their demonstrations and demands. A copy of their unofficial *Sajudžio žinios* newspaper was produced from someone's bag, and together with our Polish brother they began to take bets on whose nation might declare independence first and how the security apparatus might react.

I quickly grew bored. Their flights of fancy about how dissidents might be punished always turned out to be either too imaginative or not imaginative enough for what the KGB was actually doing. I began thinking of Žemyna and how I'd much rather spend lunch with her than listening to a group of idealists dream their impossible dreams aloud. Didn't they remember Hungary in 1956, or Czechoslovakia in 1968? This would end as all dreams of independence did in the Soviet Union.

It wasn't that I didn't want freedom and independence for Lithuania. Of course I did. I just didn't believe it could happen in my lifetime. And a ragtag gaggle of artists fantasizing and theorizing in a cheap cafe wouldn't make it happen.

I looked at my watch. I had a drawing class in the afternoon, but if I hurried, there might be enough time. I excused myself and put down enough *rublis* to pay for my share of the bill and the Pole's. Another reason my artist colleagues deigned to invite a party member like myself to lunch.

Žemyna worked in a bakery only a few blocks away. When I walked in the door, her face lit up. We were still in that phase of the relationship. She pushed her loose blonde curls away from her face, showing pink cheeks that glowed with pleasure. I guessed I still had another two months before she'd roll her eyes when she saw me arrive. She locked the front door and hung out the CLOSED sign. I let her lead me into the storeroom, where I took her from behind, against a table beside several loaves of dark rye bread.

When we were done and I was refastening my trousers, Žemyna grabbed my hand and asked, "You promised me an amber necklace, Martis. When will I get it?"

The first time I'd bought a necklace made with our "Lithuanian gold" had been for Natalie. She'd been so enthralled by the gift that I'd promised one to countless girlfriends since. Of course, I'd never delivered on those promises. Now, with the economic sanctions from Moscow, prices for black market goods had gone through the roof. A necklace like what I'd bought for Natalie could easily cost me a few months' wages. I liked my little baker and her creamy white skin, but not that much.

"Of course, Žemyna. When the protests quiet down, prices will become more reasonable. Then I will buy you everything you deserve."

She threw my hand down. "You think so little of me? Even at today's prices you would buy one for your wife."

At this, I chuckled aloud.

"Don't laugh!" Žemyna said loudly. "I hate your wife."

"Well, I can say for certain my wife would not like you either, my little baker."

Žemyna grabbed a knife from the table and waved it in my face. It was old, its handle worn, but the blade was honed to a sharpness that glinted in the dim light. "Your wife has no reason to judge me. Neither do you."

The appearance of the blade startled me. Up to now Žemyna had only shown me her sweet, gentle side. It looked like our relationship would end sooner than I'd thought. Was I losing my touch?

"I have a class to teach," I said. It was better not to let her know how much her theatrical show rattled me.

Žemyna said, "Go teach your precious class, Martynas. Perhaps I will declare my independence too."

So much for my plump little dumpling. It seemed politics was seeping into everything and rusting it out from the inside.

I had no need to dally with sweet nothings in her ear, so our tryst ended sooner than I expected, and I slipped out the back door as usual. It was at least convenient, giving me enough time left to take the trolleybus home and clean up before heading to the Institute. Natalie would be working in her lab. These days, she came home for lunch only rarely.

That hadn't always been the case. In the early months of our marriage I had used to pick her up at the lab at lunch time and bring her home, where we would make passionate love. That was before her promotion, before we'd grown bored with each other and discovered the thrill of elicit affairs. In recent years, on occasion when one girlfriend or another had been unavailable I'd called at the university a time or two, hoping to get Natalie home for lunch, but she always found a way to be too busy.

On the trolleybus I sat next to a man in a formal jacket and hat who was about the age my father would have been, had he still been alive. We exchanged greetings, but he seemed preoccupied, so I rode most of the way in silence.

As I arrived at our apartment building, I laughed to catch myself humming the *Tautiška giesmė*. It was the national hymn of Lithuania, and barely a year before it still had been illegal to sing it. We'd sung it at lunch, as my artist friends liked to do when plotting their revolution. I didn't think that singing a song would take us very far down the road to independence, but this song had a soulful melody I liked. Natalie felt differently about it. She'd recently caught me humming along to it and banned it from our home.

I walked up the three flights of stairs to our apartment and unlocked the door. I wandered into the bedroom first, kicking off my shoes and socks. Then I walked into the kitchen.

What does a man do when he finds his wife's lifeless body on the kitchen floor? Perhaps if I'd been raised on American television crime shows I would have known to scream. If we'd had BBC police procedurals to show us how to keep a stiff upper lip in the midst of our terrible personal pain and shock, I might have known to do that. Instead I did what any Lithuanian suckled at the Soviet teat would do. I stared at the unexpected in mute shock and helpless wonder.

Natalie's arms were sprawled almost at right angles to her body. Her right leg was folded up under her left. Her body faced upward, but her head was twisted to the right, her long, brown hair obscuring her face. In that moment, I knew she was dead. But some less rational being inside my head was trying to convince me that perhaps she'd only fallen. I knelt, calling her name softly, "Natalie, Natalie."

She didn't answer.

I took hold of her chin, to move her face toward me. It was cold. Her lips were blue. I slapped her cheek once, then again, in hopes of getting the blood circulating.

"Natalie!" I said more loudly.

Then I saw the blood beneath her body. I turned her over, and found the knife.

My beautiful, beloved Natalie, my loving if not faithful wife, leading physicist, respected professor and party member, was dead.

I slapped her again, and shouted. "Natalie!"

It was no use. She was dead. Staring into her half-mast eyes,

...ng them to open, I reached to take her right hand. Instead ., though, I felt paper.

Clenched in the fist where I'd sought comfort was a rolled-up sheaf of papers. I took the papers and flattened them between my own two hands. A student paper with a failing grade written on the top, beside the title: "Two-dimensional system response to unit-step input." My wife may have been beautiful and brilliant, but radiophysics was truly dull.

I glanced through the first few lines of the paper and even I with my limited understanding of science could see that the grade was well earned. Then I saw the name across the top of the page: Gintaras Degutis. My heart thudded to a stop. Degutis was a common enough name in Lithuania, but my wife had mentioned this particular Degutis to me over dinner just the week before. The son of General Mindaugas Degutis of the Lithuanian militia and a very poor student indeed.

But this was my beloved Vilnius, where no one need kill for good grades. They could be bought and sold for little more than the price of a loaf of bread. This particular young man would have had to pay far less. For a proven party member like my wife, a "word to the wise" as you Americans say, would have been enough. Like me, she was not an idealist but a pragmatist. This had been at the heart of our successful marriage.

A gentle knock at my door startled me back to reality. I looked down, surprised to see blood pooling near the cuff of my pants. What was I doing, sitting on the floor beside my dead wife reading one of her student papers? And who in the Soviet pantheon of players was already knocking at our apartment door?

TWO

IF THIS WERE ONE of your American detective stories today, I should have worried about moving the body, disturbing "trace evidence" that the police could use to cleverly track the killer. Remember, though, this was 1989, and it was not the West. The cellular phone was still the size of a brick. The personal computer was something American college dropouts played with in their garages. DNA was only a building block of life, not a harbinger of punishment for the guilty criminal.

My wife had adequate rank in the party that the investigation into her death might be more than perfunctory. The police assigned to the case might actually be competent. If the historical, political and cultural circumstances were aligned, there might be genuine interest in finding the person who'd killed her. After all, we had *glasnost* and *perestroika* on our side.

Then again, this was 1989, and the KGB had a long tradition of interfering in police investigations. They liked to use apolitical crimes to "solve" political problems, and the Lithuanian SSR was swimming in such problems just then. With Sąjūdis organizing ever more protests, with the Freedom League pushing for complete independence, and as more and more Lithuanians spoke openly about the "Soviet occupation," the ranks of "enemies of the state" grew daily.

There was the knock again, the timid knock of a supplicant, not the insistent pounding of the police. I stood, my knees aching a little from the difficulty of getting up after sitting so long on the hard floor. I looked at the clock. My class should have started already. How long had I been sitting there by my wife's dead body? I crossed through the apartment and opened the front door.

The woman who looked back at me from the hallway was, if not beautiful in a conventional sense, at least handsome and intelligent. Her eyes were a little too close together, her nose a little too upturned at the tip. Her lips were thin, but her black hair was thick and gorgeous, like Natalie's. She had piled it up on top of her head where it threatened to cascade down her shoulders at a moment's notice. She was perhaps a few years older than my wife. She wore a blue cotton dress that brought out hints of blue in her black eyes. The soft, thin fingers of her pale hands showed that she worked with her mind. When she saw me, she narrowed her eyes a little and said, simply, "Oh."

My wife was nothing if not consistent in her tastes.

"Ah, yes," I said. "You probably expected me to be at the Institute by now."

The woman shrugged.

"And your name is?" I asked.

"Indre."

I reached into my breast pocket for a pack of cigarettes. "Well, Indre, it seems that we can at least remove you from suspicion."

She leaned forward a little and pursed her lips. "What am I to be suspected of?" She spoke Lithuanian with the slightest lowlands Žemaitija accent.

"I think you did not kill my wife."

Indre's face flushed red and she took one step backwards away from the door, as if to leave. I watched her take control and hold herself very still. "What do you mean?"

I stepped aside for Indre to enter the apartment and shut the door behind her. Then I led her into the kitchen. When she saw my wife, she knelt by her side, much as I had. Unlike me, she wept. But she wept quietly, as befit her Žemaitijan reserve. I lit a cigarette and watched her through the smoke.

Men have affairs for emotional comfort, yes, but their needs are primarily physical. Affairs between women are as much about emotion as physicality. Sometimes more so. Would I weep for my little baker if I found her dead? I think not.

"Can I offer you a drink?" I took a bottle of vodka down from the cabinet and poured two small glasses. I drank one, then leaned over and took my wife's lover by the elbow, raising her up and guiding her to a wooden chair by the table. I handed the second glass of vodka to her, and poured myself another. I offered a cigarette, but she declined. We drank in silence, without ceremony.

This was Soviet Lithuania where all comrades met as equals. There were no class differences, and gender had no meaning beyond the anatomical necessities of replicating little workers to serve the state. For my wife and me, this equality had carried into the bedroom. I had girlfriends from time to time, so my wife did too. We never talked about it. It would have upset the delicate balance of our lives. As long as I was fucking other beautiful women, I couldn't fault my wife for doing the same. We'd always had the decency not to mention it directly to each other. Still, though, I'd met a few of hers before and knew she had good taste.

"Poor Natasha," Indre finally said. The sound of it was jarring. Natalie had never let me call her that. She'd said she hated the Russian sound of it.

The woman turned her glass upside down on the table to prevent me from pouring her a third glass. I finished my fourth and screwed the cap back on the bottle as she said, "You should call the police." She stood. "I should leave. This has nothing to do with me."

"How long did you know my wife?"

"Only a few months."

I saw the lie in her eyes, and wanted to force the truth from her.

"Was she as good in bed with a woman as she was with a man?"

Indre gave me a look of searing disdain that went straight to my heart. "Don't try to shock me," she said. She picked up her scarf and wrapped it a little tighter around her neck. "I'm going now. It is better for both of us if I am not involved."

A statement like that could mean anything in Vilnius. She didn't want to get involved with the police, to be sure, but why not? Because she had secrets to hide? We all did in those days, from black market radios to seditious, nationalistic thoughts. Or was it because she had killed my wife and needed to get as far away as possible? And how would it be better for me?

At the door, Indre turned to face me. "You would do well to forget me," she said. There was pain in her eyes, but it did not mask her fear.

"Do you teach at the university with her?"

Indre looked me up and down, as if measuring me for something. "I think I've been here long enough." She turned and walked out the door.

I didn't follow. She would be easy enough to find. And she was right, I needed to call the police. I needed to begin the process of solving my wife's murder. The longer I delayed, the greater suspicion would fall to me.

Our neighbor in the flat below had a telephone, and the deed was handled quickly.

"Why did you move your wife's body?" The first to arrive were ordinary police officers. They carried with them an appropriate mix of suspicion and disdain for an intellectual couple who made their living in the arts and sciences. By the time Chief Inspector Jonas Rimša arrived, the fact of Natalie's death was beginning to truly sink in.

"I suppose I was in shock, comrade," I answered. I was sitting on the living room sofa drinking tea at the insistence of the Chief Inspector who stood in front of me. His hands were clasped behind his back, and he stood a little closer than he needed to. Intimidation was, I believe, the intent of his posture. I peered around his body to try and catch a glimpse of his two colleagues man-handling my wife's dead body in the kitchen.

"Were you trying to destroy the evidence of your crime?"

"I didn't touch the knife."

Chief Inspector Rimša took a one-quarter turn to the left. "Are you having an affair?"

I looked up. For all his accusatory questions, Chief Inspector Rimša had a look of sheer boredom in his eyes. For him, this was ordinary, rote.

"Of course," I answered, hoping my plain honesty would surprise him. I reached into my breast pocket for my cigarettes. When I offered one to Chief Inspector Rimša, I saw him glance at the label before accepting. Kaunas brand, thoroughly Lithuanian.

"You will give the name..." he began, but was interrupted by a knock at the door. I started to get up, but he held out a hand to stop me and answered it himself.

You Westerners grew up with blind faith in the rule of law, so you have already filled in the rest of this scene in your minds. But I was an artist and this was the Lithuanian SSR where anything was possible, both the best and the worst. When a tall man in a well-cut dark suit walked into my den and introduced himself as Leonas Songaila from the Ministry of Internal Affairs, I could have only one thought.

A man too important for a title from the Ministry of Internal Affairs does not come for a second-rate artist and a professor of radiophysics, not even if both are party members. No, indeed. He comes for a student whose last name is Degutis. Whose father is General Mindaugas Degutis, and whose papers have been found clenched in the hands of a woman dead from mysterious circumstances.

Rimša left us and joined the rest of the police in the kitchen. Where his movements had been slow and languid before, now they were suddenly rushed and busy. The boredom in his eyes had been replaced by a dark intensity.

Songaila stared at me from across the room. "Comrade Kudirka," he finally said, "our records indicate your wife traveled to Švenčionėliai last month. How did she get there?"

"She went to see her mother. She takes the train to Švenčionėliai, then a horse cart to the village." I hoped that by volunteering too much information I might relieve his suspicion of me. Natalie's mother was a village woman who had traveled to Vilnius for our wedding six years before, and had been back only once to visit. She was a small, wizened woman, one of the rural *tuteišai* who wore peasant clothes and bathed irregularly. She spoke no Lithuanian and only a little Russian, and I spoke no Polish, so we'd had little to say to each other the few times I'd seen her. She seemed uninterested in me. She was a good cook and spent most of her time in Vilnius in our tiny kitchen cooking traditional Polish foods from her village. She cooked for my wife, really, not for me. For all that, she was Natalie's mother. My wife was quite fond of her and visited her every month.

"She makes this journey often." This was a statement, not a question, so I did not respond. If he knew this much, he would have more accurate records from the KGB than my poor memory afforded me.

Songaila looked around the room. His effort to make the gesture look casual made it seem all the more searching. When I ground out my cigarette in the ashtray he took out a pack of his own and offered me one. Gitanes. French. Imported and illegal for most Lithuanians to have. I took the cigarette, in a show of deference to the power he was displaying like a peacock waving his tail feathers.

I took a deep drag from the Gitane and found the taste unexpectedly pleasing. This, too, was intentional. Pleasure and pain. Kindness and confusion. He was beginning to succeed in disorienting me.

"What would you say, comrade, if I told you that your wife's mother died eight months ago?" Songaila asked.

It wasn't that I considered my wife incapable of lying to me. Our relationship had been built on a comfortable bed of feather-light lies. It was that this kind of lie was of a different order from the kind of lies we usually told. *I'm working late in the lab* is a world apart from *I'm taking the train to my home village to visit my dead mother for several days.*

Of course, Songaila could be lying to me, though the purpose of such a lie did not seem immediately apparent. I thought back over the past eight months. In that time I'd seen Natalie to the train station at least five or six times, each the same as the time before. She'd carried the same suitcase. She'd worn her clothes and hair with the same simple, everyday grace as always. She'd told me how she looked forward to eating her mother's *pierogi*. She'd kissed me on the cheek and had told me to be good while she was gone, with that same ironic smile I loved.

"I... I don't know what to say." I gave myself away with my spluttering.

Rather than answer immediately, Songaila walked over to a small painting hanging on the wall, a noble factory worker with muscles straining amidst a set of giant interlocking gears. I'd put a glistening sheen on the man's body and the mechanism he pressed his weight against. In truth, the image of those gears had been inspired by a Charlie Chaplin film I'd once seen, not by the official tour of the steel factory I'd been ordered to paint.

"Lithuanian Soviet realism," he said. "This is what you are known for."

"It is how I serve the people and the state," I recited.

He turned to face me. "It is garbage. Art is garbage. What is the use of art to the state?"

I shrugged. In truth, I did not disagree.

A pale young officer with bright pink cheeks rushed in from the kitchen, our transistor radio in one hand. "Sir!" he said loudly.

Songaila took the radio and turned it over in his hands to inspect it. He took his time with it, even opening up the back, popping out the battery and inspecting it. Pure Soviet theater at its finest.

"So, Comrade Kudirka. You have a transistor radio."

I put the cigarette to my lips to avoid answering, and simply nodded.

"Radio Free Europe. Voice of America. The BBC. What is your favorite?"

"We don't listen to such things."

Songaila ignored me. "Romas Sakadolskis."

"Who?" I said, though I knew exactly who he was, as every Lithuanian must. Sakadolskis was the Lithuanian voice of America's illegal broadcasts into our country. For those who were brave or foolhardy enough to listen, he shared the news of the wider world.

He often shared with his listeners a hidden world inside Lithuania, such as information about where to meet for upcoming protests.

"Don't be a fool," Songaila said. He was right. Everyone in Lithuania knew who Sakadolskis was.

"We didn't listen to such things," I repeated. Natalie didn't permit it.

Songaila nodded thoughtfully. "My colleague tells me you admit to having an affair." The sudden change in topic was, I supposed, meant to keep me off-kilter.

"Yes." This was an observable, knowable fact.

"Did your wife know about it?"

This was opinion, and thus, less knowable. "I don't think so."

Songaila's brow furrowed. "Women always know. My wife certainly does." He even bothered to color his voice with a hint of bitterness.

"Is Natalie's mother really dead?" I asked. I was beginning to regain my balance.

"I've just confirmed it with the local authorities."

Their plan was becoming clearer now. They would protect the general's son by discrediting Natalie. She would be accused of some kind of treachery against the state, a far greater crime in the Lithuanian SSR than the murder of a physicist. If they were sharing all these details with me now, they had lined up the pieces already. So quickly.

One of the policemen called Songaila into the kitchen where they conferred out of earshot. When he returned, Songaila's face had turned a deeper shade of red and his eyes were narrowed.

"Just how long did you wait to call the police?" It was as if I could see the gears turning in Songaila's evil mind. He would discredit both of us to protect the young Gintaras. Perhaps I would be blamed for her death.

"Your subordinates are already quite aware that I turned her over to try to help her. I took the papers from her hand. I am sorry that I moved her, but I had taken quite a shock."

"You drank vodka," he said, almost a shout. His face grew redder.

"She is my wife!"

"There are two glasses!"

I should have seen this coming. I should have washed and dried the glasses before calling the authorities. For a brief moment, I was distracted by the memory of Indre. I wondered if she might work in the same laboratory where Natalie did. Where Natalie had worked before today. I'd certainly never seen her at the university, those intelligent black eyes, her sweet Žemaitija accent.

I stared back into Songaila's eyes. "I poured a drink for my wife," I said. To be sure, it was a reckless move. But I didn't think Songaila cared enough to test it. His eyes were on mine, but his mind was elsewhere. He was caught up in a political calculus that included his job, his apartment and his future, as variables in a complicated differential equation.

He settled on anger. He shouted at me, "She was dead!"

"I know!" At this, I felt something deep inside of my chest collapse. I put my head in my hands and wept. "Natalie, Natalie," I heard myself murmur. My pain was as sharp and bloody as the knife in my wife's back. I wished I had one I could stab into my own heart.

Someone must have refilled my cup, because it was full of tea when I finally looked up again. I scalded my tongue on the hot liquid just to drown out the pain in my chest.

It wasn't just that Natalie's death hurt so very much. It was the way Songaila had made it clear that he did not care to search for the truth. Carrying Natalie's body out the apartment door, Chief Inspector Rimša's clumsy minions banged her torso hard against the doorjamb. One of them tried and failed to suppress a chuckle.

If there was any truth to my wife's death, I would have to find it myself.

THREE

WHEN I WOKE UP THE NEXT MORNING, it was as if I had not slept. I had not dreamt, and felt as if no time had passed since Chief Inspector Rimša and No-Official-Title Songaila from the Ministry of Internal Affairs had clomped out of my apartment with their mindless foot soldiers. Just thinking of Songaila with his chubby, pink cheeks frowning over my wife's body with one of his imported Gitanes hanging from his lips made me feel sick. Violated.

I wasn't hungry, but I hadn't eaten the night before. I made a strong cup of tea and forced a piece of dark rye bread into my stomach, followed by a spoonful of sweet bilberry jam. I replayed the facts I'd learned the night before as I smoked one cheap Lithuanian cigarette, then another.

The death of Natalie's mother was too easily disproved to be false, so it was unlikely to be a lie. This left me with the question of where my wife had been traveling to for all those months and why. But more important, why had she lied to me? All these years and months, had she been traveling to her mother's village? Had she ever been there, even when her mother was alive?

I got up from the kitchen table and went into the bedroom. When she'd come in from a trip, I'd often seen Natalie tossing her punched train tickets in a little keepsake box that stayed in the bottom of our small wardrobe.

I flung open the doors and shoved aside the clothes. There, where it should be, was the little wooden box. Her father had carved it out of pine when she was a child, nailing on the primitive little hinges himself. He hadn't been a trained craftsman, but he'd been skilled with a knife, in a rough, peasant way. He'd carved simple flowers into the lid of the box. I ran the palm of my hand across the top. The light wood was smooth with many years of Natalie's touch.

Inside the box was a conductor's dream, or perhaps his nightmare. It seemed as if she'd kept the stub from every trip she'd ever made to see her mother. All of them showed Vilnius-to-Švenčionėliai or Švenčionėliai-to-Vilnius. I began to organize the tickets according to date. The oldest was from five years ago. The most recent, last month. They were all punched, showing they'd been used. She'd been planning to go again to visit her mother tomorrow. Thinking this might be important, I grabbed a handful of the tickets and tucked them into my pocket.

Now that I had them, where should I take them? There must be someone I could show them to and say, "See for yourself—she went to Švenčionėliai, just as she said!"

But what did ticket stubs prove? Songaila and Rimša would use it as proof of whatever they had decided. I needed someone else who would see the tickets as an independent reality rather than a mechanism for achieving the goals of the state.

Indre. They had been intimate. Perhaps Natalie had told her something about her mother's death that she had neglected to tell me. Perhaps she knew where Natalie had been traveling on all these trips. I would find her and show her the ticket stubs, and ask her all the questions I should have asked my wife.

Our neighbor across the hall, Vanda Sadunaitė, must have been waiting for the creak of my footstep because she opened her door almost before I could step fully outside our own front door. "Comrade!" she shouted. She seemed to be hard of hearing. She always shouted.

Vanda was a bitter old woman who had enough curiosity to kill ten cats. Natalie and I had wondered from time to time whether she might be one of the *druzhenniki*, Lithuanian citizens who volunteered to "enforce public order." Busybodies and little proto-fascists, the lot of them.

"Comrade Sadunaitė," I answered without pausing.

I was three steps down the stairs when she shouted again, "You still owe me for the chicken!"

I turned on my heel. "Enough with the bloody chicken, Vanda!" I shouted. I couldn't bear to have this conversation again. Not on the morning after my wife had been murdered.

The sour old woman kept chickens on the roof of our apartment building illegally. One night the previous month I'd been out drinking with several artist friends. One of them, a filmmaker, had begun describing a movie he wanted to make where a man would kill a chicken with his bare hands, rip open its chest and eat its heart. He intended this as a serious commentary on the style of *glasnost* and *perestroika* being practiced by Lithuanian officials. I'd grown tired of his bluffing, and the more I drank the more argumentative I'd become, eventually saying that he'd never make this film because he was too effete and cultured to kill a chicken. Our other friends joined in, daring him to prove he wasn't.

My three friends and I had soon found ourselves creeping up

the stairs of my apartment building. It seemed I was the only one of us with access to live chickens at that hour of the night, courtesy of our wizened neighbor. The chickens had been asleep in their coop, so it was easy to capture one of them. Killing it was another task entirely. What's more, the chickens made such a racket with their clucking and screeching that Comrade Sadunaitė was soon on the roof screaming at us, four drunken artists whacking a chicken's head against the edge of the roof.

By then we had succeeded in killing the chicken. Unfortunately, it wasn't just any of her chickens, but her prized egg-layer, worth far more alive than in the pot.

I apologized. My friends apologized. My wife apologized. I tried to give her a bottle of wine and a pair of imported nylons, but she wouldn't take them. Nothing would placate Comrade Sadunaitė except for the full market price of the chicken. It was either that or a call to the authorities. I'd promised to pay, although I had no intention of doing any such thing. This was Soviet Lithuania, and surely old Sadunaitė understood that much.

In the weeks that ensued the old woman had taken to waiting by her door to catch Natalie and me as we came and went. Whenever she harangued me, I pleaded poverty. My wife and I were impecunious university professors, after all. But she knew we were also party members. I suppose she thought that if she harassed us enough, eventually we'd pay up in order to quiet her. Over time, she may have been right. Until today.

"If you don't intend to pay, Comrade Kudirka, I will be happy to call the police."

"Call the police! I don't care. My wife is dead!"

The old woman reached up toward her forehead in that ancient, reflexive gesture I'd seen many times among those of her generation. She caught herself in time though, and patted her hair instead of crossing herself.

"Was she ill?" she asked in a slightly softer voice. "How did it happen?"

The unexpectedly kind look in her eyes combined with her superstitious behavior made me angry. "With a knife in her back. Did you kill her?" Was this old harridan the type to kill over the price of a chicken?

"No, comrade." She stepped back, almost flattening herself against the door to her apartment. A strange look passed over her face. The sympathy and superstition were gone, replaced by her everyday Soviet Lithuanian suspicion. "When did this happen?"

"Why do you ask?" I said it to provoke her, as much as anything.

"I saw a man leave your apartment."

"What do you mean, you saw him leaving?" I climbed back up the stairs toward her. "When?"

"Yesterday. I heard voices in your apartment, a man's and a woman's. Arguing. I heard a man's heavy steps pounding toward the door. I waited by my door to stop you as you left your apartment. But the man who came out was not you. His face was white as a sheet."

"What did he look like?" I asked.

The woman turned wary. "Like a man." There was a teasing, almost flirtatious look in her eyes.

"Was he young? Old? What color was his hair? What was he wearing?"

"Rather younger than you, I would think."

"And?" I was almost shouting at her.

"He wore ordinary clothes. Black pants, a brown jersey. His black hair covered his eyes so I couldn't see them."

"A student! Do you think he could be one of my wife's students from the university?"

The old woman held out her hands in a gesture of ignorance. "I am but a poor working woman, comrade." She stepped heavily on the word comrade. "I did not go to university. What can I know of such things?"

"Where did this man go?"

The old woman shrugged. "He ran down the stairs. I was not looking for him, so I shut my door and left him to his business."

"Was he carrying anything?" I asked.

"Like a bloody knife? I should think I would have called the authorities if I had seen that."

"Perhaps he had a briefcase. Or something else in his hands or his pockets."

My old neighbor paused, staring at me without looking at me. She seemed to be replaying the scene in her mind. But when she came to the end, she looked me in the eyes and shook her head.

"Comrade Sadunaitė," I said, softening my voice to try and cajole her, "what time of day was it when this happened?"

"Around midday."

The time would be right. "Thank you," I said. I turned and started down the stairs. Then I suddenly came to a halt and turned back.

"Comrade, didn't the police come to you last night and ask you about all this?"

"No."

A wave of fury washed over me. If I had been seeking incontrovertible proof that their so-called "investigation" was a farce, this would have been it.

"But last night, with all the police in and out of our apartment— didn't you look to see what was going on?"

"I kept my door shut tight, comrade. These are uncertain times. I thought perhaps they were here to cart you off to the gulag."

A woman like Vanda Sadunaitė wouldn't make such a statement lightly. She was old enough to remember the mass deportations of

Lithuanians to Siberia by the Soviets in the 1940s. Still, that she said it at all, much less to a neighbor she despised, showed how much our country had changed in the past year. Lithuanians now could talk about the deportations openly without risk of prison. They were even singing songs about the deportations at some of the mass demonstrations organized by Sąjūdis. These were the signs that made my artist friends say that Lithuania would be a free and independent nation by the end of the year. Their optimism was absurd enough to make a grown man cry.

"No, Comrade Sadunaitė, they'll never take me alive." I smiled to indicate the joke.

"Please accept my condolences for your wife, Martynas," the old woman said as I went down the stairs.

Out in the fresh air, walking as quickly as my legs would take me, I could think more clearly. My decrepit old neighbor was as close to a witness as the police would find. Only the police hadn't bothered to even knock at her door. Bloody Gintaras Degutis and his impeccable pedigree.

To take this point of view, though, I had to believe she wasn't making this story up. Which was entirely possible. Perhaps the police had questioned her last night and she was telling a tall tale as some kind of vindictive torture.

Or perhaps they'd instructed her to tell me this tale, to see what information she might glean from me. If she was part of the *druzhenniki*, she'd do anything they asked. And if that were the case, I had already made one important misstep. *They'll never take me alive*. It was a joke my artist friends would have appreciated, quoting an American cowboy movie in such a tenuous moment as this. A suspicious old hag and KGB apparatchiks would make of it something else entirely.

By the time I got to the trolleybus stop I realized it wasn't Indre

I needed to find first. I had to begin with Gintaras Degutis, the student whose papers had been in my dead wife's hands. The man the police were trying to protect. The man Comrade Sadunaitė may or may not have seen exiting our apartment at midday yesterday.

Any other student would be hard to find, but men like General Mindaugas Degutis lived in houses, not apartments. They were secretive about them, but at the same time they wanted Vilniusites to see how important they were, so the location of General Degutis' house was an open secret. Like that of every other military and government leader. I boarded a trolleybus heading toward the Antakalnis District on the far side of the city, a wealthy quarter of the capital in a country where all men were equal. Except for those who were a little more so.

At least this way I could see for myself just how serious the investigation was—or was not. Had Chief Inspector Rimša shown up at General Degutis' house to browbeat the general's son into confession, to collect fingerprints and the other evidence that would prove he had stabbed my wife to death? Was Songaila there with his arrogant Gitanes?

If the police weren't there, I would do their job for them. I would take the young man's shirt in my fist and shake him until he confessed to his crime.

The house was in a quiet neighborhood filled with the homes of the *nomenklatura*. Even as we lesser members of the party were forced to live in prefabricated cement block apartment buildings, men like General Degutis were allowed to live in single-family houses. His was, for the neighborhood, average. Not too big, not too small. The yellow paint and white trim on the exterior walls were neither too fresh and clean nor too grimy.

The general's house was situated across from a small park containing a pair of run-down benches, three birch trees and a patch of brownish-green grass. A group of five young men milled about one of the benches, whiling away the day with their hands in their pockets the way young men with neither work nor schooling to keep them occupied did in those days.

I stood on the sidewalk in front of the house for some time, watching for any kind of movement behind the curtains. A shadow. A corner pulled away and replaced. But nothing. There were no police, so far as I could see. No investigation.

Some part of me knew I shouldn't do it, but my anger got the best of me, and I foolishly walked to the front door and pounded on it loudly.

No one came to the door to answer my call. No privates in ill-fitting uniforms came along to hustle me away from the great man's door. I pounded again. And again. Nothing.

It seemed strange there would be absolutely no one at home, but with the recent spate of street protests and sing-alongs, these were busy days for the militia.

I walked across the street to the park and sat down on the empty park bench. The boys hovering around the other bench fell quiet, watching me. I didn't care. They could report me or not—what did it matter? A nosy neighborhood hausfrau was probably already making a telephone call to someone who would reward her for reporting my presence at the general's house. I shook the last cigarette from my pack, lit it and took a long, deep draw. Where was Gintaras, and how could I find him?

A voice spoke to me in Russian. "If you're looking for the generalissimo, he's not at home."

I looked at the young men by the other bench. One of them watched me closely. The grave look on his face should have been comic on someone as young as him, except that he held himself with such calm intensity that I had to take him seriously. The other boys laughed and punched at each other.

It was worth a try. I answered him in Russian. "Actually, I'm looking for his son, Gintaras."

The serious young man tossed his head so that the black hair covering his eyes blew away briefly. "In that case, you should try Poland," he said softly.

"Yeah, and when you see him, tell him that he owes Pablo money," one of the other young men shouted, laughing.

A couple of the other boys shouted, "Yeah, Pablo, you tell him."

There was a flash of anger in the serious young man's eyes as he turned to the speaker. "I think our comrade Gintaras Degutis is fully aware of his debts."

The boys gave away so much with their accents. "Pablo" spoke Russian not as Lithuanians did, but as a Russian. The boys with him had the voices of native Lithuanians. I wanted to admire Pablo and his tough, cool indifference, but couldn't. My heart was filled with the instinctive dislike we Vilniusites had for our oppressors and the sycophants who surrounded them.

I asked, still in Russian, "Doesn't the general give him money? How could he owe anything to common street trash like yourselves?" I was being deliberately provocative to this "Pablo."

There was a slight pause while the boys looked to Pablo to determine how they should respond. When he smiled, they laughed. "The general is a bastard," one of the boys said in Lithuanian.

Another piped up, "He doesn't give anything to anyone, least of all his layabout son who hangs around with the wrong crowd." He said this in the voice of an old Lithuanian man.

This had them all doubled over with laughter. All of them except Pablo, who only continued to smile. He stared back at me. I felt hairs on the back of my neck go up.

For all I hated about this boy who called himself "Pablo," I believed in his inner strength and powers of observation. I stood and approached him. "Poland?" I asked softly. "Why? When?"

"About an hour ago," Pablo lowered his voice to match mine. "We were here waiting for Gintaras when a military jeep rolled up. The generalissimo raced out of the house with his wife and son. The wife's hair was still in curlers. General Degutis climbed into the jeep. Wife and Gintaras got into in their little blue Volga with another soldier driving them. I heard the driver of the jeep tell the other driver not to stop for anyone or anything until they reached Pasiekos."

"That's on the Polish border," I said.

"Exactly."

"What kind of suitcases did they carry? Small bags for a short trip or large bags for a long trip away?"

"Nothing at all, which I think means they were planning a very, very long trip."

I nodded. Their departure was abrupt and unexpected, and they didn't want the neighbors to know they were leaving. "Do you know why?"

Pablo shook his head. "All I know is that Gintaras left without paying the money he owes me. When I see him again, I'll give him a beating he'll never forget."

I didn't doubt it.

With General Degutis and his family gone, I had only one place to turn, which was where I'd begun my day. I had to find Indre.

My wife most likely would have known her either from one of the scientific laboratories or from her work with the party. The third alternative was some kind of lesbian underground in Vilnius. They had all sorts of other undergrounds, one for people who listened to Frank Zappa records, one for pagans and one for those who planned political demonstrations against the Ignalina nuclear power plant. An underground for teetotalers and another for people who drank moonshine in abandoned factories. So why not one for lesbians? But my ability to access this particular underground would be limited for obvious reasons. It also seemed a bit too risky for my wife. Her loyalty to the party may have been driven entirely by pragmatic professional ambition rather than ideological belief, but that ambition was very real. For that reason, I doubted she would let her hair down in that milieu either.

I decided the science lab where Natalie had worked was the best place to start. I took the trolleybus to the industrial district of Žirmūnai, only a short distance away. Then I walked the final blocks to an unmarked modern building in the Soviet style. Its bland, cement block exterior camouflaged what my wife had many times assured me was "some of the most exciting radiophysics work taking place in the Soviet Union today." Better than some of what the Americans were doing even. In the early days of our courting when I asked for details, she'd smiled prettily and reminded me how it was generally better not to know certain things.

When we were first dating, I'd met Natalie here on several occasions for lunch or at the end of her working day, but I'd never been any farther than the front lobby where a steely receptionist and two armed guards kept Soviet science safe from prying eyes.

They remained in place even now, as implacable as ever. I set my lips in a firm Soviet line as I approached.

"I'm Martynas Kudirka. My wife is Dr. Natalie Milosz." If the police were busy building the evidence to match their conclusion about Natalie's death, then they might not have made it out to the science lab yet. In case they had, though, I did not want to be caught asking to see a woman I knew was dead.

"Comrade Dr. Milosz is not in today," the receptionist said.

This did not necessarily mean she did not know about Natalie's death.

"I know. I am here to pick up some of her things." Still no lies they could catch me in later.

"I am sorry, Comrade Kudirka, I cannot let you into the building.

"Is Indre in today?" I ventured.

"Dr. Indrė Bučienė?"

Aha. I was right, and now I had her name. "Yes," I said.

"Comrade Dr. Bučienė is in. What do you want with her?"

Typical Soviet paranoia. "Perhaps she can retrieve my wife's things for her."

The old battle-axe looked me up and down with undisguised disdain. No, the word "old" is unfair here. I would place her in middle age, but her ugly green military uniform and the way she wore her ash-blonde hair pulled back in a severe bun added years to her apparent age. The shelf made by her large bosom resting on the desk recalled to me childhood memories of running between my grandmother's enormous industrial brassieres as I played among the laundry lines in our small backyard.

"Comrade Dr. Bučienė is working in her laboratory and has asked not to be disturbed."

So she was in. I knew I wouldn't get any farther with this woman. Still, I had to put in the effort, if only for show. If I went away too easily, it could raise her suspicions.

"Please, comrade. Couldn't you just let Dr. Bučienė know that I am waiting? If she chooses not to see me, I will leave."

She folded her arms across the shelf of her chest. "You will leave now."

I hesitated for a moment, as if considering whether to argue. Then I shrugged and said, "As you wish, comrade. Good day."

I walked back toward the trolleybus stop and took a place in line at a nearby newsstand. I had waited for Natalie many times in this very same place, back in the more hopeful days of our relationship.

There were more newspapers and magazines on the stands than there had been for many years. It seemed every Lithuanian with an opinion felt a compulsion to put it into print. I picked through them one by one, flipping to this page or that at random. The range of opinions in them ran the gamut. Everyone had a different view on *glasnost* and *perestroika* and what they meant to the Lithuanian people. The Artists' League was using those terms to redefine art, even as the historians' associations used them to rewrite history. Half a dozen other people stood browsing at the newsstand. Unsure who they might be, I finally settled on a long-running, middle-of-the-road publication. I bought the paper and a pack of cheap Lithuanian cigarettes, then stepped into a small café on the corner where I could drink a coffee, read my paper, and keep watch on the entrance to the building where my wife had worked when she had been alive. It was nearly eleven in the morning.

I read slowly and methodically, pacing myself for a long stretch in the cafe. As I watched, a few people trickled in and out of the laboratory, many more in uniform than I remembered from the old days. My wait was barely more than a quarter of an hour. Indre emerged from the building wrapped in a jacket that was too warm for the weather. She looked down, intently studying the pavement in front of her as if to be ready lest it leap up and attack her at any moment.

She appeared to be headed for the trolleybus stop. I paid for my coffee as she passed by my window. I walked out the door and stepped into rhythm with Indre's pace. Once we were out of earshot from the crowd at the newsstand I took her arm to stop her.

"Indre," I said softly. She looked up, startled.

"Oh. Yes. You."

"Her mother was dead," I said softly. "Did you know that?"

Indre frowned. "Yes."

"For how long?"

"For how long what?" she asked. "How long has her mother been dead, or how long have I known it?"

Her question put me off my balance. "Both, I suppose," I said. She stared at me until I settled on an answer. "How long have you known it?"

Hands still in pockets, Indre tightened her arms against her body. "I was questioned about her four months ago by men from the KGB. They told me she was traveling to see a dead mother. They asked me to keep an eye on her, report her activities."

"Did you?"

"A request like that," she said, "what would your answer be?"

True, there was only one correct response to that kind of request.

"So you spied on her."

Indre looked down at the pavement and did not answer. In a strange way, Indre as my wife's spy seemed more intimate than lover. This made me feel very much alone. It wasn't only that I hadn't really known my own wife; I hadn't even traveled in her closest inner circle. It was stupid and foolish of me, but I felt excluded, and it hurt a little. The security services had never bothered to question me. Because they trusted me so much, or so little? Had they known better than I had, just how far apart we had grown?

"What kinds of things did you report about my wife?" I asked.

"Nothing important, and very little that was true."

In the strong outdoor light, I saw something in Indre's face I hadn't seen the night before. A scar, thin and sharp as a razor blade, ran along her left cheek and chin. Without thinking, I reached up to touch it. Indre jerked away quickly.

"Yes, your wife said you were a whore." She turned and walked up the sidewalk quickly. I almost had to jog to catch up.

When I was alongside her again, I asked, "What does 'nothing important' mean?"

"I told them stories," Indre said, never slowing her steps. Keeping up with her almost left me breathless, but she seemed not to feel it. "Natalie and I used to construct them together. Where she had been, who she had seen, what she had done. In bed, it was fun, a game. When I actually had to meet with the KGB agent to tell the stories, it was terrifying."

A teenage boy suddenly ran past us, jostling me hard. "Sorry!" he shouted without stopping. Several papers flew free from a stack on his arm. I picked one up. A sheet of paper. Across the top in all capital letters were the words BALTIJOS KELIAS, "Baltic Way." Below that was a drawing of three hearts that met at their points. The print was black and white, but anyone would know that the design of the stripes across each heart represented the national flags of the three Baltic nations. Around the hearts were the names of the leading pro-independence groups in those countries: *Vilnius Sąjūdis*, *Tallin Rahvarinne* and *Riga Tautas Fronte*.

Below that, a date: 1989-08-23. A date every Lithuanian had seared on his heart, the fiftieth anniversary of the Molotov-Ribbentrop Non-Aggression Pact. The agreement between Stalin and Hitler when they had divided up East Central Europe between themselves even as World War II raged. The Germans had given Lithuania to the Soviets.

"We will be free of the bloody Russians soon," Indre said, looking over my shoulder at the paper.

I wadded up the paper and threw it into the gutter. Had she been asked to spy on me? Report to the KGB where I had been, who I had seen, what I had done? At least in this case I could reply with my honest opinion. "No. It's hopeless," I said. "The Russians will never leave the Baltics. No amount of singing or protests will ever change that." In our country, folk songs had long been a tool of popular resistance against our overlords, be they Russian, German or Polish. They had made us strong and helped us to persist as a people, but had they ever made our enemies leave?

"Did you read the piece about the Baltika Song Festival in yesterday's edition of *Literatura Ir Menas…*" she began in a low voice, but I cut her off by stepping in front of her to force her to stop walking.

"We are talking about my wife here, not about the lies they print in the newspapers!"

"Your wife believed in the songs," Indre whispered. At first I thought I had misunderstood, because Natalie believed no such thing.

"That is a story you made up to tell the KGB."

"No," Indre said. "She was working on an article about the importance of keeping scientific endeavor free from the influence of the Party. For the Lithuanian Scientists Union."

"That's not possible. Natalie is a party member!"

Indre shrugged. "So are half the members of Sąjūdis."

This was true. Many of my artist colleagues were skeptical of the leading Lithuanian reform party for exactly that reason. Artists I knew supported the more radical Lithuanian Freedom League instead.

"Natalie's article was very important and it simply had to be published. That's why we had to make up stories to tell the KGB."

This didn't sound anything like my pragmatic wife. What good would publishing an article about scientific freedom do? It would make her a target, nothing more. Still, Indre spoke with authority. What else did she and my wife do together? "What about those trips to visit her mother? Did you two lie in bed and make up that story too?"

Indre paused. "She told me she was visiting her mother's village. It was the KGB who told me otherwise."

I ventured a guess. "Songaila?" The man without a title from the Ministry of Internal Affairs.

"Yes."

"What did Natalie say when you asked her about what Songaila had said?"

Indre shook her head. "I didn't want to know, so I never asked. It was safer for both of us."

I dug into my pants pocket and removed a handful of train ticket stubs. "Look at these. To Švenčionėliai, the train station nearest to her mother's village. All of them." I handed them to her.

"What do you expect me to do with them?" Indre asked.

"I have a right to know what my wife was doing!"

"I don't think you do. It's clear, you hardly knew her."

It seemed Indre might very well be right.

"Give me a cigarette," Indre demanded, her voice suddenly an urgent whisper. I tore open the new pack and shook out two, put them in my mouth and lit them both. When I'd given one to Indre, she said "Look in this shop window with me."

I turned to look into the window of a bookstore, as barren as any shop in the Lithuanian SSR. Five books sat on display in the window. A hardback history of Lithuania in Russian. A beige and brown Russian-English disarmament dictionary. A tourist guidebook to Vilnius in English, with a photo of an ugly office building on the front, its colors fading to blue in the sun. The biographies of Marx and Lenin looked fresh off the presses. I noticed with surprise that Stalin was missing from the triumvirate.

"There's only one, but he's been following us for three blocks at least," Indre muttered.

"Where..."

"Don't turn around!"

This was the era of *glasnost* and *perestroika*, yet here we stood staring into a shop window trying to figure out how to escape a security tail. I was a mid-level artist of some minor repute. My wife was dead. We were party members, for god's sake! But we did have our own KGB. Even if they weren't investigating my wife's murder, her death had drawn me into a circle of suspicion.

Or were they following Indre?

We stared into the window. I pointed at one of the books by way of a ruse and said softly, "They're following us, instead of investigating her death."

"I know." Her voice was sandpaper, rasping and bitter.

"Let's go to the village. Let's find out what she was doing there."

Even in her blurry reflection in the window, I saw a brief spark of interest light Indre's eyes. It disappeared as quickly as it had arrived. "How can we find out anything? Do you speak Polish?"

"There will be at least a few Russian speakers there. Anyway, it's a small village. We ask for the mother, we ask about Natalie. Someone will tell us."

"What do you think you will find there?" Indre asked. She narrowed her eyes as she sucked in smoke.

"Indre, they're not going to investigate her death. Not a real investigation. They're just looking for someone to pin it on. Me. You. A Sajūdis member they need to put behind bars."

"Why do you think I would go with you?"

"Because you loved her," I said. Either that, or because she wanted to report to her KGB handlers. It really didn't matter to me which. I may not have loved my wife enough to know her in life, but I was started to realize that my desperate desire to know the truth of her death might be its own form of love.

"No, you want me to go because you want to fuck me," Indre said.

I shrugged, to flatter her. "But I won't."

"You won't try because I'll cut off your balls."

I let that hang in the air a moment. The image was disturbing, but also arousing.

"He's probably been following me all morning," I said. "Let's split up. You go into the bookstore and buy something while I head for the train station. If he sticks with you, can you lose him?"

"Of course," Indre sneered.

"Good. I'll do the same if he follows me. Natalie's ticket is for one-thirty this afternoon. We should buy our tickets separately, then meet up on the train."

Indre nodded.

I said, "Don't go home. Lose him and get to the train station in time for the one-thirty train to Švenčionėliai."

"But I don't have anything for traveling," Indre said, her perpetual scowl deepening. "Not even a toothbrush."

I shook my head. "They've seen you with me. By now, they may have set someone up at your house to watch for you."

"All right, then," she said. "I will see you on the train." With a brisk, sudden movement she reached for the shop door and walked in. When the door had shut behind Indre, I continued down the street. I told myself not to keep my hopes too high of seeing her again.

FOUR ➤

I HEADED TO THE BAKERY, thinking my little Žemyna would give me both escape from the man following me and a moment's sexual release that would give me courage. Beside Indre, I had felt unexpectedly weak and incompetent.

Žemyna greeted me sweetly, seeming to have forgotten our little tiff the day before. I unfastened my pants and went through the motions, but the sad woman in my mind's eye was sometimes Natalie, sometimes Indre, each a little dusted with rye flour. In the end, I found myself unable to perform. Žemyna was kind, but I could read the frustration in her eyes. As we tidied ourselves up, I looked around the room for the knife she'd waved at me earlier. I spotted it on a table at the back.

"What time did you come to work yesterday?"

Žemyna looked up from retying her apron over her skirt. "You know a baker begins the day early. I was here at four o'clock in the morning."

"Did you go out at any time during the day?"

"What is this with all these questions, Martis?" She reached under the cabinet and took out a bottle of honey mead. "Perhaps this will help." She poured the mead into two glasses and held one out to me.

Žemyna as murderer? It was possible, but it seemed so unlikely. Comrade Sadunaitė had seen a man leaving our apartment in the middle of the day. When I had been here taking my pleasure with Žemyna in the afternoon, my wife was already dead. And here was the knife itself, on a table in a bakery rather than in my wife's back.

"It's nothing, my little dumpling." I took the glass she was offering and raised it in a toast to her. She raised her own glass back to me, and we both drank deeply.

I hadn't heard the front door to the bakery open, so I was startled when a man walked into the back room. The bakery manager, Žemyna's boss, looked from Žemyna to me and back again, then to the bottle of mead. He dropped a small stack of papers down on the table beside us.

"No flour?" Žemyna asked.

He shook his head. "You cannot buy shoes in Vilnius, but they make sure we have our drink to keep us weak and stupid." He made a disapproving face.

Žemyna turned to me and rolled her eyes. "Adolfas is temperance."

"Put that bottle away," Adolfas said, his voice firm and angry. "We've talked about this before."

Žemyna's face went red, and she slipped the bottle under the cabinet without recapping it. I was curious that he seemed more concerned about a simple bottle of mead than a strange, disheveled man in his kitchen. This man's attitude was based in nationalism rather than puritan values, I decided. Some of my friends had joined the temperance movement and stopped drinking as a protest against the Soviets. Alcohol weakened us, they said, and they urged sobriety as a way to hasten the day when we Lithuanians would rise up against them.

Humorless bastards, the lot of them. If there was going to be an uprising, I wanted mine the way Emma Goldman did, with dancing.

"I should go," I said, and headed for the door. Neither Žemyna nor Adolfas said a word to try to stop me.

I exited quietly through the hidden back door and took a roundabout way to the train station. It would take some time before the man following me would realize I'd given him the slip.

When Indre walked onto the train and sat down beside me, the relief I felt told me how worried I'd been that she wouldn't come. In her right hand she held a book wrapped in flimsy brown paper. As she settled in beside me, an old man in the seat across the aisle scowled at us in the Lithuanian comradely manner.

"Which book did you buy?" I asked.

Indre carefully unwrapped the package: a history of the Lithuanian Communist Party. I took it and flipped through the pages, mostly to show anyone who might be watching that we were an ordinary, dull couple who'd been together long enough to be well past the need to converse. I ran across an early painting of mine in the book, a man and a woman standing in traditional Lithuanian clothes, their four hands grasping a flagpole. Atop the pole was the red hammer and sickle flag of the Soviet Union. The couple looked upward and into the distance, toward a bright Soviet future. Completely derivative and unoriginal, as was all my most popular work. Only, I'd swapped out the nose, lips and jaws of the models who'd stood for the painting. The man in the painting had the lower part of the woman model's face, and vice versa.

As we waited for the train to depart the station, time stretched out until it began to seem like forever. The ride to Švenčionėliai would take about an hour and a half, and would make eleven stops before our destination. Indre stared past me out the window, still but alert, seeming to pay little attention to the bureaucratic formalities of a Soviet rail departure.

When we were finally out of the station and well on our way out of Vilnius, Indre closed her eyes and relaxed. Before long, she dozed off. The swaying of the train rocked her head to the side, against my shoulder. Still playing the role of the considerate husband, I put an arm around her. Indre did not stir.

I must have dozed off too. As we pulled out of a station stop I was awakened by the movement of Indre shaking herself out from under my arm. I looked through the window to get my bearings. We were departing Pabradė. Only two more stops before Švenčionėliai. I followed Indre's gaze as she quickly scanned the compartment. The old man was gone, and most of the closest seats around us were empty.

"I told you to keep your hands off me," she whispered harshly. Her hair had come loose, and she reached up a hand to shake it free.

"Just playing the role of kind and gentle husband," I ventured, putting on my best, most tender smile.

"Where do you think you are, some South Sea island? This is the Lithuanian SSR. We don't have kind and gentle husbands."

Had I been a kind and gentle husband to Natalie? In the early days, perhaps, when our love was fresh as little yellow rue buds. So much had happened since then.

"I went to see General Degutis this morning," I said, keeping my voice low.

Indre leaned back a little in her seat. "That took balls. What did you find out?"

"They've left."

"Who's left?"

"General Degutis and his entire family. They've pulled up stakes and left for Poland."

Indre frowned. "Why?"

"These days, who can tell?"

Indre frowned. "You talked to the general? Or Gintaras, the murderer?"

"They were gone by the time I arrived, but there were some people watching the house."

"KGB?"

"No. Apparently Gintaras isn't very clever with his money and he's borrowed from some rather unsavory characters."

Indre looked alarmed now. "I hope you haven't drawn attention to yourself. People with money can be worse than the secret police."

"Believe me, I know," I said, even though I didn't. "Pablo was Russian through and through, but most of the kids with him were Lithuanian."

"Pablo? What kind of Russian name is that?"

"I'm not stupid. Obviously it's some sort of *nom de guerre*."

Indre pressed the fingers of her right hand into her forehead and shook her head a little. "You learned his fake name; he learned your real one."

"No, I...." but I couldn't remember. Had I told Pablo my name?

"Why didn't you tell me about all this before?"

"I'm telling you now. It only happened this morning."

Indre's face turned pink and her pupils dilated like a cat preparing to attack a small bird. "I knew I shouldn't have come on this train with you. I don't care if you get yourself killed or put in prison, but I'm a fool if I let you take me with you."

"But if we don't find who killed Natalie, no one will."

"Keep your voice down!" Indre said in an urgent whisper. "And stop saying people's names out loud as if you wanted to incriminate them!"

"I have to say her name. It is all I have left of her."

She pressed her lips together and looked away sadly. I reached over and took her hand. Indre snatched it away.

"Natalie described you perfectly," she hissed.

I turned toward the window with a jerk and crossed my arms. I didn't want Indre to have memories of Natalie. I didn't want anyone to. She had been mine, and I wanted her to stay mine forever. I stared into the dark pine forest and forced myself to think about how I could mix paints to create just the right shade of green to capture it. I did not want to think about Indre and Natalie together.

The train slowed as we approached the Švenčionéliai station.

"Oh, I can just see you in the classroom," Indre said, "putting your arm around the shoulder of a pretty little girl to guide her hand and show her how to make this paint stroke, just so, careful to brush up against her breast gently." She rubbed her arm up against mine to demonstrate. It was true enough. I did not answer.

Shuddering and bucking like an old mule, the train pulled up to the platform. Indre stood abruptly. "Let's go."

We stood side by side on the platform. I took out two cigarettes and lit them. I handed one to Indre.

"What will we do now?" she asked.

"We need to find transport to Natalie's village."

Indre sighed. "Why don't you go sort that out? I have to visit the washroom."

I hesitated. Had she changed her mind? Would she bother to come back from the washroom? No, that was ridiculous. For all her severe posturing, she had come here for someone she loved, as I had. Anyway, even if she decided to sneak away, where could she go in this little backwater of a town?

"Sure," I said. We walked into the station together. I passed through the exit, in search of a car or a horse and cart, someone who might care to take us to the village for a few *rublis*.

Two small cars were parked on the street, both unoccupied. The two people who had disembarked from the train with us were walking into town in two different directions. Half a block away, a woman in a red checked kerchief was on her knees, tending to flowers in front of a house. Beside her, a brown dog drank from a ditch.

A man in brown pants and a blue shirt stepped out from behind the station and walked up to the pale yellow car.

"Comrade!" I called out. He turned. "I need a ride. Can you help me?"

"It's too far," he said, even before I could tell him where I wanted to go. He slammed the car door shut, started the engine and drove away without a second glance at me. I lit another cigarette.

The station door slammed behind me, but when I turned, no one was there. I peered into the window, and was shocked to see my wife standing in the middle of the station. Her back was to me, but it was her all the same. "Natalie," I whispered. My heart pounded in my ears.

It only took a split second, but I realized it wasn't Natalie. It couldn't be Natalie. I knew Natalie was dead because I had found her lifeless body with a knife in it.

The woman turned a little and I saw her profile.

Indre. I'd seen a hint of it when she'd stood in my apartment the day before, but now, with her dark hair down, at a little distance, the resemblance was remarkable. Beside her stood a blond man with wide shoulders. On the other side stood another man, this one smaller and darker. The dark man took her arm while the blond spoke to her. What man wouldn't want to talk to such a beautiful woman?

Then again, they could be KGB. Indre could be making her report. That's why she'd sent me on to arrange a ride.

But when the blond man put a hand on her elbow and tugged at it, Indre pulled away. The other man grabbed hold of her other arm with both hands. Soon all three of them were walking toward a door at the far side of the station.

Indre's hair flew as she jerked out of their grasp. She made it two, three steps away before the blond grabbed her from behind by both arms. She spun around, looking for something. For me, perhaps. Even from that distance I could see the fear in her eyes. The two men took a firmer grip on her from either side and began walking her away. A moment later, they turned a corner and disappeared with Indre.

FIVE

I SCANNED LEFT AND RIGHT as I ran into the station, nearly tripping over a small, sobbing child who'd sat down in the center of the room. A gaggle of spirited young people in matching red and gold tracksuits walked in behind me. Ahead of me, a door was closing. I ran for that door.

The men had taken her down a side road. Together they moved with jerking, sideways motions even as they made surprisingly quick forward progress. The figure on the left had blond hair, the one on the right, brown. In the center was the woman who looked remarkably like my wife.

They moved her along the sidewalk like professionals. Some kind of law enforcement, or worse, secret police. Indre struggled against them, but they held tight and kept pushing her forward.

My first instinct was to run up to them as fast as I could, tackle the two men, then escape with Indre. But I lacked the physical and mental confidence required. My second and more intelligent instinct was to close the gap between us somewhat, then follow at a safe distance. I was unlikely to win any physical argument with these men. I could only hope they did not have a car waiting for them somewhere.

We turned left, moving into the heart of town. We'd made it five blocks along when the men suddenly came to a halt in front of an old six-unit apartment building that edged up against the sidewalk. It was the kind of building the Soviets would have torn down in Vilnius to replace with dull gray cement block edifices. Indre lost a pretty black patent leather shoe as they dragged her up the three steps to the front door. The blond held her arms pinned behind her back as the darker man unlocked the door. They opened it and pushed Indre inside.

I stopped just short of the apartment building and stood very still, trying to decide what I should do next. The air was heavy with the smell of onions and cabbage roasting in one of the apartments. An old woman in a hand-knitted gray sweater eyed me suspiciously as she lumbered up the street with a string bag heavy with vegetables dangling from her right hand. I looked away from her and reached into my pocket. Cigarettes would give me a purpose standing alone on a street corner. But they were gone. I must have dropped them at the station. I couldn't stand on this quiet street much longer without attracting attention.

So I began walking as slowly as I could toward the front door of the building. As I approached the entrance, a curtain in one of the downstairs windows fluttered, and I caught a brief glimpse of her and the blond man. She was sitting in a chair. He was standing over her, his angry red face close to hers. The shorter man with dark hair stood back at a little distance. I sidled up with my back against the wall and leaned one ear toward the window. I couldn't see into the apartment, but I could make out words if I focused.

"...kind of trick?" the blond was shouting.

"I tell you, Natalie is dead!" Indre shouted back at him.

"Why did you kill her?" A different voice. The other man, the one with darker hair. His Lithuanian carried with it a notable foreign accent. Not Russian or Polish. Not Eastern at all, which would explain the way he'd thrown his shoulders back inside the wide shoulder pads of his jacket as he'd hauled her up the street. This darker man was from the other side of the Iron Curtain, and he knew my dead wife. In that terrible moment, I thought my heart would stop.

"I did not kill her!" Indre shouted.

There was the sound of a slap. Indre made a grunting, sobbing sound.

I turned to look into the window, but the curtain had settled and I could not see. I hadn't any choice. I picked up Indre's forgotten shoe, then took all three steps to the front entrance of the building with one leap. To my good fortune, they had left the door unlocked.

Inside the hallway, the dank building was in a typically Soviet state of disrepair. Near the ceiling the bare, gray walls were laced with cobwebs and stained with mildew. Several rails on the sagging banister that led to the second floor were missing or cracked. I tiptoed to the door of the ground floor apartment where they were torturing Indre. Holding my breath, I stood outside and listened carefully. I could hear the rolling cadences of an angry conversation, but I could not make out words. If I wanted to know what they were saying—if I wanted to find out what they knew about my wife—I would have to get inside the apartment.

A loud wail sounded through the door. Indre's voice. Had she refused them? Were they killing her?

A composite image from American films watched illegally in friends' apartments passed through my mind: Dirty Harry in dark sunglasses with a Rambo kamikaze bandana tied around his head and a pistol in his hand. I was not that man, but in this moment I must act as if I were. Without a second thought, I lifted my foot as high as I could and punched with all my might at a spot beside the doorknob, as I'd seen so many times in those American films.

The door didn't budge. I fell back, pain shooting from the heel of my foot all the way up into my knee. Indre's shoe fell from my hand as the door opened and the dark-haired foreigner lunged at me.

I'd lost the element of surprise, but I kept my head. I had Eastern wiles to play against his Western brute force. I stepped aside as the foreigner overstepped, then I ran in through the door. I saw a table. I grabbed for something on it, anything. The Westerner was coming at me from behind. I turned and swung at him wildly with the heavy, metal item in my hand, focusing every ounce of strength in my body on him. To my surprise, it connected with flesh and he staggered backward a few steps. I looked down to see a heavy silver picture frame in my hand. When I looked up, the foreigner was holding the left side of his head with his hand.

The blond Lithuanian moved toward me next, but my clever Indre kicked out her feet and tripped him. He tumbled to the floor in a heap, only to jump up again and come at me even faster.

Before I knew it, the Lithuanian had the picture frame in his hands and the foreigner had his arm wrapped around my throat. The apartment door was closed again. The foreigner held my body close to his like a lover and spoke into my ear from a very close distance. He didn't shout. He didn't need to.

"You're lucky you didn't do any worse damage," he said. "If I were to end up on a slab in the basement of some godforsaken Baltic hospital, people would find you. People you don't ever want to know." His Lithuanian grammar and vocabulary were quite good, despite his terrible accent.

He squeezed my throat a little tighter and shouted, "Who is this man?"

Indre stood on her own two feet now, but the Lithuanian was holding her arms twisted behind her back. She tightened her lips and stared at the Westerner blankly. The Lithuanian answered for her. "That is Martynas Kudirka, Natalie's husband."

How did he know who I was?

"Ah! The famous artist," the foreigner said, pressing his manhood a little into my buttocks. "Maybe he killed his wife in a fit of jealous rage," he said.

I felt my face growing red from a lack of oxygen. "I am not a jealous man," I choked out. "Please. I cannot breathe."

Indre spoke quickly. "Martynas and I are traveling to see Natalie's mother. The old woman at least deserves to hear the news about her daughter from a friend." Indre's ability to lie convincingly under pressure was breathtaking. I would have already confessed all if I weren't being strangled by a capitalist ape. "Now please let us go. We will not make any more trouble for you."

To my surprise, the blond Lithuanian let go of her arms. "I don't think this woman knows anything about Natalie," he said. "Not anything important."

"Are you really so stupid?" the foreigner answered.

The face of the Lithuanian went pink, and he raised his voice. "You don't know my people as well as you think you do."

The foreigner sighed. "Maybe this one's girlfriend did her in." He let go of me with a shove. I found myself half leaned over and gripping the arm of a loveseat, gasping for air and grasping for the truth. I was truly rattled. Had Indre told them about Žemyna? How could she have known about my little baker? No, she looked as lost and confused as I felt.

Which made the situation far more frightening. These two men knew about Žemyna from someone else. I stood up straight and stared at the blond Lithuanian man more intently. Had I ever met him? Had I ever seen him on the streets of my beloved city?

"The only reason I'm here is to pull Natalie out and get her to safety," the foreigner said. "She signaled us. She had collected all the papers, but she thought she'd been compromised. Now she's dead. We have to assume the worst. She's dead and you two are here. What do you expect us to think?"

Compromised? My Natalie? She was much worse off than that.

"Who is *we*?" I asked. "Who are you? You're not Lithuanian." My brain was sluggish from the lack of oxygen, but I was beginning to get an idea of who he was, and it did not sit well with me.

"I'm your best friend, if that's what you want me to be." The smile on his face was anything but friendly. "Or your worst enemy." He reached up and rubbed the angry red lump that had appeared on his left temple. At least I had done that much.

Indre said, "Only an American would be so smug and self-assured in this situation." The three of us turned to look at her. She raised her chin as if daring the man to disagree with her. "He is one man in a foreign country, and we are three Lithuanians. We could do anything to him, and who would know?"

The American—I agreed with Indre on this point—turned to the Lithuanian. "This is getting messy. We should get rid of them before they can report us."

"No!" The word was out of my mouth before I had time to consider whether it was in my own best interest to speak.

In the time it took me to regret my impulse, the American had taken a pistol from his pocket and aimed it at my forehead. I broke out into a cold sweat and my knees went weak beneath me. "Remember, buddy, you called us," he said to the Lithuanian. "If this all goes to shit, it will be on your head, not mine."

"You don't have to kill him," Indre said. She twisted around to face the Lithuanian and said, "Make this stupid American shut up, and we will cooperate. What kind of papers did Natalie have for you? We will find them."

The blond walked over and placed his hand on the pistol. "No more dead Lithuanians," he said. "Not today. Not even for democracy."

Democracy? My Natalie was killed for cheap Western ideology?

"Put the gun away now," the Lithuanian said. His voice remained still and even, but it sounded yet more angry than before.

My throat was dry and sore, and my legs felt as if they were made of water. I wanted desperately to sit down, but I dared not. I had to stay strong.

"You can't shoot them here," the Lithuanian said to the American. "You'd have half the nosy old biddies in Švenčionėliai here within moments."

The American shrugged, then lowered the pistol and shoved it in the waistband of his pants at the small of his back. He looked at Indre, then back to me. "Your wife loved her country."

"I know that better than you do," I whispered.

The Lithuanian said, "She wanted us to be free."

"You would free us from the Soviets by handing us over to the Americans?" Indre asked, gesturing toward the foreigner. "Is subservience so engrained in the Lithuanian spirit that we can't imagine freedom without first prostrating ourselves before some kind of foreign master?"

The American shrugged. "Your people came to us."

"I suspect you made yourself conveniently available," Indre said.

"We love peace and freedom," he said.

"Call it whatever you like. What you love is money and power."

"Enough! She was my wife!" I shouted.

They all turned and looked at me.

"What was she doing? Why had she come to meet you? Where

were you going to take her? You," I pointed at the foreigner, "you are an American spy, but I cannot imagine what you are." I spat this last at the Lithuanian man.

He stepped forward and put out his hand. "My name is Antanas. I am with the independence movement."

The American broke in. "Goddamn it, you Balts are all the same. Give away the farm over some sentimental sense of your blighted nation."

Antanas turned on his heel. "I've had enough of you and your Cold War posturing, Kurt. This is my nation. These are my people. I will tell them what I want!"

The American whose name was Kurt threw his hands up in frustration and walked a few paces away. He stared back at us, hands on his hips.

"Do either of you know anything about the papers?" Antanas asked.

"What papers?" I asked. Indre shook her head. I believed her. The confusion on her face looked sincere.

"Natalie was supposed to bring the papers today," Kurt said. He pointed at Indre. "I don't think it's any coincidence that a woman who looks so much like her takes the same train on the same day to the same place, with the dead woman's husband. You killed her and destroyed the papers. You've come here to find us and report us to the KGB."

"What papers?!" I said. "We don't know anything about any papers!"

Antanas looked at Kurt, who looked away, shaking his head.

"The Soviet Union is on the verge of collapse," Antanas said. A short, involuntary guffaw sounded in my throat. Indre gave me a look of such searing disdain that I coughed a little to cover it up. These people were incorrigible, but I wanted to get out of Švenčionėliai alive.

"Lithuania is in the lead," Antanas continued. "The Freedom League is pressing to declare independence from the Soviets, but

Sąjūdis and some of the larger pro-democracy groups aren't willing to go so far."

"They are afraid of what real freedom might mean," Indre said.

Antanas nodded. "These papers Natalie had collected, they show the true history of some of our current leaders of Soviet Lithuania. What they did to sell us out to the Germans during the war. The names of tens of thousands of people they sent to work to death in Siberia. Other crimes since then. We will use these papers to convince them to give up their opposition to independence."

"Blackmail," I whispered.

"Perhaps," Antanas said. "But already it is beginning. See?" He took a sheet from his pocket and unfolded it. It was a faded copy of the same paper we'd seen earlier that day, when a boy running past us had dropped it in the street. BALTIJOS KELIAS, it read, and a drawing with three hearts that met at their points.

He handed the paper to me. "In two days, on the anniversary of the treaty that gave the Baltics to the Soviets, we will line up in the streets all across our three nations," Antanas said. He leaned in closer to Indre and me. "We will create a human chain stretching from Tallin in Estonia to Riga in Latvia to Vilnius in Lithuania. People will line up across more than six hundred kilometers, standing side by side to demand their freedom. Our freedom."

If enough people show up, I thought. If the police and militia and KGB don't drive everyone away. Aloud, I asked, "What do you honestly think will come of it?"

"We will force Sąjūdis to declare our independence from the Soviets." The sparkle in his eyes was genuine, and the urgency in his voice made it almost seem possible. "It is why we need those papers. With our enemies inside the current government silenced, our dissident allies will grow more bold."

"You paint a pretty picture," I said. "You even make me want to believe in it."

Antanas said, "Those papers Natalie had, they are a crucial piece of the puzzle. Our country needs them."

We all stood in silence. Whatever the others might have been thinking, my thoughts were of my wife and what a terrible husband I must have been to know so little about her.

Kurt looked at his watch and said, "The last train back to Vilnius leaves in less than two hours. We have to be on it. These *kvailiai* don't have our papers, so we need to come up with a new plan." He started buttoning his jacket.

"No, I think Martynas and Indre could help us," Antanas said.

"They're useless! If they tried to help, they'd only screw things up." He took the picture frame I'd used to smack him on the head and replaced it with remarkable precision on the table.

"They deserve a chance to participate in one of the greatest moments in our country's history."

Kurt turned his back to Antanas and spoke directly to us. "Go home and go back to your meaningless lives. Stay away from the independence movement and for God's sake stay away from the demonstrations. We'll keep an eye on you both, and if we see anything funny going on," he looked me straight in the eye, "we'll drop a dime on Indre to the KGB, tell them she's feeding secrets to Romas Sakadolskis at the VOA."

I looked at Indre, who shook her head and rolled her eyes. She didn't seem frightened at all.

For myself, I was too tired and confused to argue. None of this made any sense. Natalie had always been the first to dismiss the protesters who sang Lithuanian songs in the streets as naïve and ungrateful. Whenever she caught me accidentally humming one of them as I washed dishes or painted—which couldn't be avoided these days as the songs were in the air around us all the time—she would get angry and announce I was forbidden to sing them.

I'd thought I'd understood her. Natalie loved Lithuania as much as I did, but she came from a family of Polish peasants. To her, the nationalism of those Lithuanian songs represented a dangerous bigotry and hatred. Her faith in the ideals of international socialism was pragmatic, rooted in the simple human need to survive, and maybe a little bit more. That was what I'd always believed the Party meant to Natalie.

I might have misunderstood my wife, and I am certain I underestimated her. Still, whatever else Natalie might have believed in, this Kurt with wide shoulders, his bullying stance and a pistol in his pants could not have been one of them. But if she had been working with these men, that work must have meant something to her.

Kurt told us to leave the apartment first, that they would follow at a safe distance. Indre and I did as they said. We paused at the door where Indre's shoe had fallen. I held out an arm for her to balance against as she slipped it back on.

We walked back to the train station and managed to buy tickets for the last train to Vilnius. I kept my promise not to look back to see if Kurt and Antanas were following, but I did glance into the windows we passed along the way from time to time, lingering for as long as I could. I occasionally caught the reflection of the two men in the glass.

Indre and I were quiet for most of the trip back. The heat of the day had leaked away, and we leaned into each other for comfort as much as warmth. By the time we arrived back in Vilnius station I had an arm around Indre. She was wide awake, smoking and staring into the setting sun on the other side of the window. I tried to imagine that we were alone in the carriage, that nothing in the world existed but the fields and forests we passed, the lone crane standing imperiously on one leg in the middle of a little lake, and the tiny brown flycatchers that flitted past our window.

As instructed, I let Indre off the train first. I shuffled about with a newspaper and shoelaces to the count of one hundred, then stood up. I made my way slowly up the aisle. As I stepped off the train, my willpower weakened and I turned to look back. Antanas was standing only two rows behind where Indre and I had sat in silence all the way from Švenčionėliai to Vilnius. His face seemed drained of color, the whites of his blue eyes wide and round. Kurt was still in his seat, sleeping, it seemed, his head lolling over to the side at an uncomfortable angle.

We were the only ones remaining in the coach. Antanas rushed up the aisle and did not stop, pushing me off the train ahead of him.

"Keep moving," he hissed as we stepped down onto the quay. "Find Indre and meet me at the Neringa. Kurt is dead."

I'd been to the Neringa a few times with artist friends. It was a popular restaurant on Gedimino Avenue, known for its jazz concerts and good food. It seemed a strange place for Antanas to choose. It was exactly the kind of place the militia and KGB would come looking for no-goodniks making trouble against the state, like him.

When we arrived, though, I saw how it was the perfect place to meet him. Packed and noisy with a throng of patrons that spilled out onto the sidewalks, it would be hard to find any one particular dissident or malcontent. We joined the crowd milling outside the restaurant.

Antanas walked up and then past us. We followed at a distance. He continued past the entrance and around the corner. In the dark of the side street, I could make out a few spectral groups of people from the glowing ends of their cigarettes. As we grew closer, their bodies solidified into the shapes of ordinary men and women. We joined Antanas where he waited for us in the spindly shadow of a maple tree.

"You killed him," Antanas said abruptly.

First my wife, now Kurt. If Gintaras turned up dead, no doubt they would point the finger at me. Perhaps they would blame me for all the murders in Vilnius that summer. "That's not possible," I said. "I wasn't anywhere near him."

"The picture frame," Antanas said. "Something in his head must have come loose when you hit him. He was perfectly fine, then he went to sleep on the train and never woke up."

"Maybe he wasn't dead," Indre said.

The glowing end of Antanas's cigarette moved from one side of his mouth to the other. "I know dead, and Kurt is dead."

"You poisoned him. Something in his drink, or an injection," I said.

Indre jumped in quickly, "Yes, how do we know what you were doing behind us in the train?"

"Why would I want him dead?" Antanas said. "Kurt was here to help me get Natalie safely out of Lithuania."

I turned to Indre. "Did you know Natalie was going to leave us?"

She shook her head. "I had no idea."

"She was in danger," Antanas said. "The KGB were on the verge of taking her in. Killing her was extreme, even for them, but these are extreme times. Now we have nothing. No papers, no Natalie. And now no Kurt, thanks to you."

"Is Kurt from the CIA?" Indre asked.

"Something like that."

My stomach turned over. I'd already guessed his true identity, but to know for certain I had killed an American spy terrified me. I should get some kind of medal from the Lithuanian SSR. Instead, I found myself standing in the dark conspiring with an enemy of the state.

"If you're thinking about turning me in and collecting some kind of reward," Antanas said, strangely reading my mind, "you should first consider that you are under suspicion for your wife's murder. You should also consider what the Americans will do to you when they find out about this. Kurt wasn't officially here, so there will be no need for his colleagues to note in their official records whatever they might do to you."

"Shut up with your idiotic threats," Indre said. She sounded undaunted. She threw back her shoulders a little. "We are here because we loved Natalie. She gave her life for something she believed in. To honor her memory, I will finish the task she began. Tell me about the papers."

I was stunned, and yet I was not. Indre had already proven she was made of sterner stuff than I. No wonder my wife had loved her. I felt stupid standing there in the dark, a simple artist trying to live a convoluted Soviet life. These women put me to shame. It was as if they spoke a language I could barely read, and could not speak at all.

Antanas said, "We haven't seen them for ourselves; she described them to us. There are official documents that connect some of the current leaders in the Lithuanian Communist Party to atrocities in the 1940s, '50s and '60s. Some date all the way back to World War II, showing men who later became Communist Party leaders, colluding with the Nazis to send Jews to the camps."

"How did she find these papers?" Indre asked.

Antanas said, "I don't know. I never asked because I didn't want to know, to keep myself safe. Now I wish I had. They were a critical part of our plan."

"What plan?" Indre asked.

Antanas took a deep drag of his cigarette, then tossed it to the ground and stepped on it hard. "Sąjūdis has done good work organizing the people, but they have taken the middle road for long enough. We were going to meet with some of their key people in advance of Friday's demonstration. Once they see the evidence, we are certain they will finally be emboldened to release an official statement demanding independence. At the same time, our contact in the Ministry of Internal Affairs is arranging for meetings with some of the leaders who are implicated in the documents. We are equally certain this will convince them to quiet their rhetoric against the independence movement. Some of them may decide to leave the country quietly, while they still can."

"Songaila," I said. The man with no title who had shown up at my house to "investigate" Natalie's murder.

"You know him?" Antanas asked.

"He had Natalie killed," I said.

"No, he's one of us. On our side."

I shook my head. "Never."

"We have tested him," Antanas said. "We are certain."

"He isn't even investigating Natalie's murder! He's planning to pin it on me. Or on her student, Gintaras Degutis, if that doesn't work out."

"You have it all backwards," Antanas said. "If he isn't investigating, it's to keep from exposing her. That's the only reasonable explanation."

Indre asked, "Where do you think the papers are?" Her focus was relentless.

In the distance, a whistle blew. An overnight train was leaving Vilnius. I should have stayed at the station. I was a fool not to be on that train, wherever it might be going. Anything would make more sense than standing in the dark talking with this man.

"We don't know. She didn't tell us and we didn't ask. In your home, Martynas? In her office? Some other safe hiding place?"

I'd given the police free run of the house the night before. I'd sat in the living room smoking Songaila's Gitanes while they'd searched everywhere. If those papers had been in our apartment, they could have been found already.

But if Songaila had found them and was on the same side with Antanas, we wouldn't be here now. He would have delivered the papers to people in the independence movement.

Indre said, "Gintaras could have been her source for the papers. His father would have had access to all sorts of secrets in the militia."

Antanas nodded. "If that's the case, then the general might have had her killed to keep his son from giving her the papers." He shifted his weight from one foot to the other. "No, Gintaras would have given them to her already. If that's what happened, then the general spirited his family out of the country so his son's treason wouldn't be uncovered."

At least that made more sense than killing my wife over a bad grade.

"Unless the general himself is the source," Antanas added. "Sąjūdis now has more silent support from government officials and the military than you might imagine. Perhaps Natalie was killed after his son delivered the documents, and Degutis fears his family is next."

I threw my cigarette butt to the cement and ground it with my heel. "And perhaps Songaila is actually a CIA operative! This is giving me a headache. God alone knows who's on whose side. Welcome to Soviet Lithuania!"

"Soon to be free Lithuania," Antanas said. "If we can get the information we need. So much depends upon those papers. Indre, do you think you find them?"

"I can look in her laboratory and her office, and a few other places I know. Perhaps she hid them in my apartment."

"I don't think she would have put you at such risk."

"No," Indre said. "I think not. She was a kind and generous woman."

They were talking as if I wasn't there at all. It was infuriating. "That is my wife you are talking about!" I shouted.

"Hush, Martis," Indre said softly. Her use of the diminutive was disorienting.

Antanas had harsher words for me. "Don't go getting us killed, idiot," he said. Then he turned back to Indre. "When you find the papers, call me on this number. Find a telephone in a place where no one knows you."

"You are the one who is going to get Indre killed, Antanas," I said.

"She's a smart woman, and she knows the risks," he said. He looked her up and down as if measuring her for a coffin. "She knows how to take care of herself."

"Bloody hell," I muttered.

"I'll probably need to search your apartment," Indre said. "Give me the key and I can do it while you are teaching. Or perhaps while you are with your girlfriend."

"I'll search my own goddamn apartment!" I said. I wanted to shout, but kept my voice low. It sounded thin and bitter in my own ears.

The two of them stared back at me.

"Are you sure?" Antanas said.

I had said it aloud in a fit of pique, and even as I spoke, it had come true. To my surprise, I wanted to search for those papers. I wanted to find them. I wanted to be the hero my wife had been. "Yes. I'll find these papers wherever she's hidden them and I will deliver them to you and your benighted revolution."

Indre reached over and took my hand in hers. Her fingers felt cool and soft as they gave a gentle squeeze. "It's what Natalie would want," she said.

I took a deep breath. Indre was right. Natalie would want someone to finish her work. Now that she was dead, there was so little I could do for her. "I can do that much for Natalie," I said.

"For freedom," Antanas said.

"For Lithuania," Indre whispered.

SIX

FROM THE NERINGA, each of us took a different direction. I doubled back a few times, circling blocks I didn't need to circle, just in case anyone might be following me, friend or foe. Then again, I wasn't sure if I'd be able to tell the difference, one from the other.

As I crept up the stairs of our apartment building, part of me expected to find the door thrown open and members of the KGB rummaging through the accoutrements of my life. I lifted the door up on its hinges as I opened it in order to make as little noise as possible. But there was no one there. I felt both relieved and a little disappointed.

Sitting down at the kitchen table with a small glass, I took two quick turns of the bottle. I needed something to keep me company on my search. Our home was small in the Soviet way, but Natalie was a scientist, and she was clever. If the papers were in the apartment, it could take me a very long time to find them.

With the first glass, I toasted Natalie. The second was for Indre. With the third, I decided I would begin my search in the bedroom.

Not because it seemed the likeliest place to hide stolen government documents, but because it seemed to have the fewest places to hide them. Also, if the neighbors downstairs heard me moving around in the bedroom late into the night, that might arouse suspicion. They were less likely to hear my late night scufflings and scrapings in other rooms.

I started with our clothes cupboard. We'd inherited it from Natalie's paternal grandmother who'd told her it dated back to the early 1900s. Made from oak, it was a dark reddish brown, heavy and ridiculously ornate for the austere functionality of the Soviet era. I took all the clothes down from the top shelf. Nothing underneath them. I shook out each shirt, blouse and pair of pants before refolding it and returning it to its place. I hadn't asked if I was looking for a few sheets of paper or a whole sheaf. How big would the packet be? How old? I really didn't know what I was looking for at all.

Nothing there. I even went through all the pockets. I found some small bills and change, all of it in *rublis* or *kapeika*. No foreign money, no secret documents.

Then I turned my attention to the dresses and coats hanging in the cupboard, shaking each one out, rummaging in pockets. When I came to the beautiful blue dress with little yellow flowers that Natalie had worn to our wedding, I discovered that I was weeping. I buried my face in the dress, but the scent of her was gone. Instead, I smelled cheap Soviet laundry soap straight from the factory. I wrapped the silky fabric around my neck and sat down on the floor with the bottle and glass. I toasted the dressmakers of Jurbarkas and the soapmakers of Klaipeda. I toasted Stalin, Lenin and Snieckus. Then I went back to work.

When I'd exhausted the options inside the cupboard, I searched the nooks and crannies at its edges, in the back, at the bottom. I dragged the cupboard away from the wall by a few centimeters and ran my hands all along the back of it. Nothing pinned up or stuffed into a space where two pieces of wood didn't quite meet. This was, after all, a very well made piece of furniture from a time when Lithuanian craftsmen took pride in their work.

I searched the bed and Natalie's small dresser with the same care. I ran my hands along every inch of the walls and floors, tugging without success at ill-fitting boards wherever I found them. By the time I was done, the vodka bottle was down by one-third, and it was past midnight.

Our tiny bathroom was a much simpler affair, but the kitchen took me until two in the morning, and the bottle was nearly three-quarters gone. Still nothing. Not even the slightest hint of Natalie's secret life that I'd just learned about.

The sofa, tables and chairs in the den were cheap, modern and Soviet, so they took less time to search. Half a dozen of my paintings were leaned up against the wall in one corner, and I began removing them from their frames. My drunken mind conjured up an image of Natalie taking one of them apart one day to hide documents behind the canvas. She would have chosen the one in dark, shadowy yellows and greens showing a little boy looking up in wonder at the bright red Soviet flag fluttering above a gleaming steel tractor. The boy held a half dozen flowering sprigs of rapeseed in one hand. Natalie had secretly loved that painting, though she'd never said so directly. We'd agreed early in our marriage that we would not have children. For Natalie, it was a pragmatic decision in support of her career, but I knew she secretly wanted a child. As for me, I did not like children and the decision was an easy one. I toasted the little boy and his red Young Pioneers neckerchief.

When I was finished with the paintings I ran my hands over walls and floors of the whole room. Nothing, nothing and still more nothing. With the last drink from the vodka bottle, I toasted Natalie again, tears streaming down my face.

The next thing I knew, I was waking up to the pink-tinted sunshine of early morning stealing in through the windows. I was face-down on the floor, my head turned uncomfortably to the side so that my right cheek was pressed against the edge of our little rug.

I slowly lifted myself up and made my way into the bathroom to vomit. I stripped off my clothes and bathed in ice-cold water, brushed my teeth, then climbed back into bed naked. Nausea rumbled, and my failure to find the documents weighed heavily on me. They weren't in the apartment. I should have known Natalie would be more clever than that. More kind, even, than to put me at risk. Or did she trust me so little?

It didn't bear thinking about. My last thought as I fell asleep was to hope that Indre would have better luck at the laboratory.

The cheap, tinny sound of the Lada car horn in the streets woke me with a start. I glanced at my watch. One-thirty. I blinked against the bright light that filled the bedroom. One-thirty in the afternoon, it meant. Slowly, it all came back to me as if I were remembering a bad dream. The search for the papers. The train. Kurt, the dead American spy. Natalie, also and forever dead.

The worst of my hangover seemed to have passed, leaving me only with a halo of headache wrapped round my head. I was ravenously hungry and desperate for coffee. Also, I had promised to meet Indre near the laboratory to share with each other what we had found in our searches.

I dressed quickly. My movements around the apartment were clumsy with distraction and hurry. As I was locking the door behind me, a voice called out behind me.

"Comrade Kudirka."

The old woman.

"Vanda," I said. I took a deep breath and turned to face her. I was too exhausted to make the effort at polite words.

"While I am sorry about your wife, there is still the matter of the chicken."

My god, was she to give me no peace at all? To ward her off, I smiled rather than spoke. It didn't work.

"Today, comrade," she said. "If you do not pay me what I am owed today, I will bring in the authorities."

Her words meant nothing to me now. My dead wife had turned out to be in league with an arrogant Westerner I had killed, our nation was on the verge of revolution, and this woman wanted money for a chicken. What worse could she do to me? I stared back at her stupidly.

"You think that being the painter Martynas Kudirka will save you, but let me tell you, I know people too."

There was something different in her voice this afternoon. A firmness and certainty suggesting a knowledge I should fear. If she was one of the *druzhenniki*—perhaps even if she wasn't—it was possible Vanda Sadunaitė could in fact do much worse to me.

Then I had a sudden realization that hit me like a punch in the stomach: Someone was protecting her. Those chickens on the roof were too loud to be a secret. If that same someone found me with the documents I was seeking in my hands, even just caught me talking to Antanas, my life wasn't worth the canvas upon which I'd painted my last picture.

"Today," she said. "I want my money today." The sparkle in her eyes suggested that today she would prefer to see me suffer the consequences of failing to deliver.

"Yes, today," I echoed, then turned to descend the stairs. All the way down, even out the building and into the streets, I could feel the old woman's eyes on my back.

Indre was already at the newsstand when I arrived. Two crushed cigarette butts at her feet suggested she had been waiting some time. The first words out of her mouth went directly to the point. "You didn't find anything either."

I felt myself sag a little. "No."

I picked up a newspaper and flipped through it. *Komjaunimo Tiesa*, the popular newspaper of the Communist Youth League. Even the official organs such as these were becoming more outspoken in support of democracy and freedom.

"I've been through everything," she said. "Files, desk drawers, little hiding places in her office and the lab. Nothing."

I paid for the newspaper and we walked away from the newsstand. The harsh squeal of tram wheels taking a turn too quickly sounded in the street, startling both of us to a halt. What was the rush, I wondered.

"We promised him papers," Indre said.

I turned back to look at her. "We only promised to look."

Indre sighed.

I answered her sigh. "There's nowhere else to look."

"There's her office at the university," Indre said.

"But there are so many people at the university who might see me. They will wonder what I'm doing there."

"She was your wife! They would expect you to collect her belongings."

"The papers won't be there," I continued.

But Indre heard between the lines. She leaned in close and spoke in a subdued voice. "Yesterday, you said you cared. About Natasha. About our country."

"Yes," I admitted, ignoring that angry little voice in my head that hated the way Indre called her that. "I do."

"Think of the sacrifices men like Antanas and Vytautas are making for Lithuania."

"Vytautus?" Who was she talking about now?

"My god, Natalie said you kept your head in the sand, but

really!" Indre said. She paused, waiting for me to understand her, but all I could do was shrug my ignorance. "Landsbergis!" she said in a loud, impatient whisper.

Of course, the founder of Sąjūdis. I said, "We are in a sad place if our country's greatest hope for the future is a bloated, self-important music professor."

Indre frowned. "All you have to do is go to her office this afternoon and clean out her belongings like any good widower would, and possibly change the course of history. Few people are given an opportunity like this."

I shook my head. "But tomorrow is the…" I paused to construct a euphemism for the human chain across the Baltics planned for the next day. Unable to come up with anything clever, I referred to it as, "the big event."

"Exactly! Every policeman, soldier and intelligence officer is busy with preparations, following all the known troublemakers, even Chief Inspector Rimša and your Leonas Songaila from the Internal Affairs Ministry. A widower going about some rather mundane tasks will be ignored. Even if someone follows you to Natasha's office, you will only be doing the ordinary things any man would do under the circumstances."

It dawned upon me slowly, an awareness of how precarious my position was. An expert hunter couldn't have laid a better trap for *Homo sovieticus* than the one I found myself in now. On one side of me stood Natalie, with Indre and Antanas and their bloody papers. Perhaps Songaila along with them. On the other stood Rimša, Vanda Sadunaitė and her godforsaken chickens, and whoever was protecting her. Surrounding them all were the KGB, the *druzhenniki*, the militia of General Mindaugas Degutis and some unnamed American spy agency. Whichever way I turned would be a pathway to disaster.

Indre rolled her eyes. "Men. You give up so easily."

"It's not that…" I began, but Indre cut me off.

"I understand," she said. "You're a famous painter. You're doing fine under the Soviets, and you're in mourning over your poor, beloved wife. Why bother trying to change anything?"

"No," I said. Like any true Lithuanian patriot who knew our country's history of domination by one neighboring power after another, I wanted nothing less than freedom from the Soviet Union. I wanted so much to believe everything she said.

"Don't you see? Tomorrow, everything changes," Indre said, almost in a whisper. "That change begins here, in this city that you claim to love so well."

My beloved Vilnius. If I believed in nothing else, perhaps I could believe in that. If Vilnius was to be an epicenter of a great uprising against the Soviets, then I had to be part of it. For Natalie, if not for myself.

"All right," I said, knowing even as I said it that there would be a terrible price to pay. I was ready to pay it, to walk into the trap with my eyes wide open. "I will do it."

Indre smiled. "And I will come with you."

Something sad in her smile made me want to protect her. The feeling shot through me like a spear. "No, I'll go to her office tomorrow. You should stay home," I said.

"Why?"

I said, "With such a large demonstration, it won't be safe on the streets. Not for you, not for anyone."

"I'm a big girl, Martis."

In that moment, the thing I needed to know most of all was that Indre would remain safe from harm. I reached out and grabbed her hand. "Promise me you won't be part of the human chain."

Indre slipped her hand out of mine, shaking her head. "I don't make silly promises to stupid men."

So much could go wrong. Yes, the militia and the KGB and all the other instruments of state security would be focused on tomorrow's troublemakers, but there would be time for the quiet payback of old grudges. What if I was one of the "little problems" someone decided to clean up? What if Comrade Sadunaitė's protectors came after me?

"Don't go," I said.

Indre didn't answer. She simply kissed me good-bye on each cheek and turned away with that heartbreakingly sad smile. I watched her down the block until she turned a corner. Then I turned in the opposite direction and headed for home.

When I stepped off the trolleybus at the stop nearest to my home, a woman was standing there with three chickens in her hand. She wore a traditional red and black plaid peasant dress, covered by a white overskirt and a matching plaid vest. One didn't see such clothing very often in Vilnius. Her clothes were worn but clean. She'd covered her head with a blue kerchief with tiny yellow flowers all over it. It reminded me of Natalie's dress, which I think is what caused me to pause, and gave me an instinctive sympathy for this woman. Her eyes were small, her cheeks red and a little sunken. She looked to be older than me, but it could be difficult to tell about village women. All that hard work in the summer sun and bitter winter cold aged them quickly, but their physical strength and endurance could be magnificent in bed, if they hadn't been cowed into sexual timidity by puritanical village mores.

Her chickens were tied together at the feet. The woman held them by the legs so that their heads hung down almost to the sidewalk. I thought of being upside down myself, of the discomfort of blood rushing to my head. The chickens were docile, eyes blinking stupidly, but otherwise they were still.

The trolley must have passed through recently, because we were the only two people at the stop. "Eh, comrade," the peasant woman said. "Will you be in Cathedral Square tomorrow?"

"You mean," I said, then paused. Was the trap about to snap

closed on me? No, I couldn't believe that. "Have you come to Vilnius to be part of the human chain?" I asked.

"I want to see the Soviets leave with my own two eyes," she said, her mouth twisting in anger. "They killed my father when they deported him to Siberia in 1948."

"Let us hope for freedom for Lithuania," I said.

"Freedom for all the Baltic nations," she answered. One of her chickens shifted and made a sound that was halfway between a cluck and a gurgle. It made me think of Vanda Sadunaitė and I found myself growing angry again. Then I had an inspiration.

Vanda didn't really want another chicken. She had plenty of them and could probably get as many more as she needed from her village relatives. What she wanted was cash. But every time she harassed me about it, she said it was a chicken she wanted.

"Mother, are you selling those chickens?" I asked.

The village woman looked from side to side. I couldn't help but follow her glance.

"I could be," she said.

"How much for one?" I asked. "The smallest one."

The woman grinned, showing several missing teeth along the top. The ugliness of her dentition erased the innocent peasant beauty I'd thought I'd seen in her face. I looked away, focusing instead on the chickens as she sorted through them.

We came to an agreement on the price quickly, as one did when negotiating illegal transactions in the streets. When she untied the chickens and handed me the one I'd purchased, it flapped its undersized wings listlessly, then settled down.

"Ach, Martynas," Vanda said when I held up the chicken in front of her. I'd practically run up the stairs to her apartment so that I could knock on her door before she'd have time to hear me coming.

"Your chicken, Madame," I said. "As promised."

She prodded at the chicken to inspect it, a sour frown on her face, but she did not take the bird from me.

"A healthy specimen," I said. "Fresh from the country today."

The old woman glared at me. She knew what I was doing, and I knew she knew. But I left her with no choice. She wanted compensation for a dead chicken; now she had it.

After another moment's hesitation, Vanda took her keys from her apron pocket, then closed the apartment door behind her and locked it. "Come with me, and bring that scrawny capon with you."

I followed her up the rickety narrow ladder at the end of the hall that led to a door in the ceiling. We walked across the roof single file to the coop, where she unlocked the padlock. The chickens inside the coop rustled around a bit, clucked gently, and settled back down. I placed the new chicken inside the cage with a flourish and untied its feet. The poor bird stumbled about, trying to right itself. I imagined all the blood now rushing from the chicken's head, back down into the rest of its body. I hoped it wouldn't give the bird some kind of stroke.

"Comrade Sadunaité!" a voice called up the stairs. It was one of the other neighbors on our landing.

"What is it?"

"Something is burning in your kitchen!"

"My dinner!" the old woman shouted, and ran for the stairs. She paused only briefly and yelled back to me, "Make sure he gets to his feet before you come down. And lock up the coop behind you!" Then she disappeared down the ladder with remarkable speed.

The other chickens clucked at the intruder, but they didn't seem terribly interested in the new arrival. The bird was still struggling to find his feet.

"Hello, my pretty little chickie," I cooed. "Be good and settle in so the old battle-axe will stop harassing me."

The poor, disoriented chicken got himself wedged into a far corner of the coop underneath a small shelf, and seemed unable to turn around. He banged his head against the shelf above his head. Then again, and again.

Even our chickens had grown suicidal in the Lithuanian SSR. "Don't go dying on me now, chickie-chickie." I leaned in through the door, reaching over to try and help him. When I did, I caught sight of something white peeking out from the wall. It was only visible from underneath the shelf. Curious, I reached for it. It was tucked in well, but not too tightly. When I tugged at it gently, a sheaf of folded papers came loose and slipped out from between two boards in the chicken coop wall.

The papers had been pecked at on the corner that had been sticking out. Otherwise, they were in good shape.

What was Comrade Sadunaitė hiding here? I flipped through the papers quickly, eager to find her hidden secrets. Now I would find out who her protectors were. I'd know to whom she might report me.

Some of the papers were recent, but many of them were old. Too old. Something wasn't right. Many of the pages were yellowed with age, the dates on them going back to World War II.

Then I saw certain familiar names. Famous names. Official seals and stamps. Then the names and seals seemed to proliferate. There were too many people from too many parts of Lithuanian officialdom.

No, this wasn't about Comrade Sadunaitė at all. I crammed the papers into the interior pocket of my jacket and stood up straight, staring out over the red tile rooftops of Vilnius. I shut the door of the chicken coop, slammed the padlock home and rushed down the ladder as quickly as I could, my heart beating wildly.

I had found my clever Natalie's documents.

SEVEN →

PERHAPS ESPIONAGE COMES NATURALLY to some men. I would have expected it to come easily to me. Sneaking around with other women so that Natalie didn't learn of my affairs had been so simple. A white lie here, an evasion there. Slipping out of clothes late at night in the kitchen. Treading carefully to avoid certain squeaky floorboards. Turning corners at just the right moment to make sure I wasn't seen by this friend or that.

Making sure one wasn't followed when taking incriminating documents to independence activists was another task entirely. I had no training in this.

I suppose some part of me had always justified the way Natalie and I had sneaked around behind each other's backs as our own personal protest against the petty invasiveness of the state. Now I realized that I'd merely been cheating on my wife, while she had been doing the kind of espionage I could only dream about. It made me feel cheap.

There was something more terrible I had to consider: perhaps Natalie had loved Lithuania more than she loved me.

If she did, then at least I knew that about her now, if I could not have known it when she was alive. I had joined her ranks and become a dissident. I had to act as she would have. The first thing I had to do was find a public telephone far away from my home, my work and the usual paths I traveled.

No, the first thing I had to do was hide the papers in the apartment. I stood in the middle of our bedroom, looking up and down for the right place. Where had Inspector Rimša's men searched and where had they overlooked? I should have paid better attention. I wrapped the papers in a shirt and stuffed them far into the back of the bottom dresser drawer. Then I took them out, unwrapped them and placed them in between two of the paintings leaning against the wall of the den, next to the sofa. They slipped down the frame, where the edges of the paper were visible from below. So I took them out again and rolled them up to place them into a tall, narrow, rusty tin that had once held spaghetti noodles imported from Italy. But they were too big for the tin.

In the end, I folded the documents into a pair of undershorts that I folded into a sweater, then placed between two other sweaters on the shelf in the clothes cupboard. Then it was time to find a telephone.

Antanas had given us instructions, a number to call and a code to speak. I needed a telephone in a busy place, but one I didn't ordinarily frequent. At least my years of marital infidelity had taught me how to find telephones to make surreptitious phone calls. But I thought it best to avoid the not-too-far-out-of-the-way places I'd used in the past to call my girlfriends.

I decided to try the Užupis District. When my father was young, it had been home to a thriving Jewish community that was later decimated by the Nazis. During the Soviet era the area had been left to its own devices and had grown derelict. With the winds of *glasnost* and *perestroika* blowing through Vilnius, artistic types looking to get away from stultifying Khrushchev apartment blocks had started moving to Užupis. It was still run down, the sort of place where you would look for the things you wanted and just might find them if you had enough cash. Every good citizen of Vilnius visited there from time to time, seeking things we couldn't get through legal means, or for things that had gone missing and we hoped would turn up at a price we could afford. But many other people would go there with other secret agendas. I wouldn't stand out.

There was a fairly direct route to Užupis, but I took three different trolleys and a bus to get there, trying to imagine how my wife the spy might have done it. First I went north, then east, then walked all the way back to the trolley line I'd started on and went south five stops past the one nearest to our apartment. As the trolleybus was about to pull out from the fifth stop I suddenly looked at my watch and jumped off. I rushed to the other side of the bus shelter as if I were running for the bus, but in fact I wanted to shield myself from view. Standing still, I could feel the sweat trickling down the sides of my chest from my armpits. I tried to make myself look like an ordinary citizen, but my eyes darted this way and that. When I was fairly sure no one had followed me, I walked across for the bus to Užupis.

Once there, I headed down the main street, then took a narrow side street into the heart of the district. I stopped at a corner canteen where I ordered bread and cold *šaltibarščiai* soup that I did not want, and a half-bottle of vodka. I stood at the counter and poured vodka into my glass. It took me three shots to get my ragged breathing under control. I dipped the bread into the cold beet soup and chewed on it for form's sake. The other men and women in the canteen stared into their soup bowls, so I did the same. There was little conversation, but what talk there was created a surprisingly loud cacophony of echoes, bouncing from tile to cement and back again.

There was a telephone in the corner, near the cashier. I poured the last of the vodka into my glass and drank it off, then headed for the phone. As I walked toward it, I rehearsed in my head the lines Antanas had told me.

But when I arrived at the phone and put my hands in my pockets, I realized I'd just spent my last coins on food I didn't want and vodka I didn't need. I looked at the cashier. She was a young thing, blonde, but with dark eyes and a narrow nose. A Nordic look, with a little Polish accent. There were plenty enough of her type in Lithuania. What set her apart, though, were the terrible acne scars across her cheeks and forehead.

I held out the smallest bill in my pocket. "Can I get change for the telephone?"

She ignored me as she rang up a customer who was also buying soup, bread and a half-bottle of vodka. Probably three-quarters of her customers all day would buy the same thing. The only alternatives were a beet salad and full bottles of vodka.

When she was done with that customer she turned to me and took the bill from my hand. She pocketed the bill, and placed a single coin in my hand. Exactly enough for a local telephone call and only a quarter of the value of the bill I'd given her. She glared at me, her eyes daring me to ask for the rest of my change.

With a prettier girl, I might have teased. With an old woman, I would have flirted shamelessly. This girl's face made me sheepish. Clearly, she had done this countless times before. This was the way she got back at a world that was so ugly to her.

I let her win. I turned my back to her and lifted the handset off the phone, hoping my call would go through on the first try. I had only one coin.

"Yes." The voice on the other end was brisk.

"Good evening, comrade," I paused as I gathered myself up to speak the code as I had been instructed. "I am calling about my booking for Palanga. Is there any news?"

The Baltic Sea beaches of Palanga were a popular spot for vacations among people across Eastern Europe. It was easy to get permission to go, but difficult to get train and hotel reservations. They sold out months in advance.

"We should know tomorrow afternoon. Would you like to come by the office? Perhaps around five p.m."

"Okay," I said. I would meet them at five tomorrow evening.

"I assume you will bring payment with you," he hesitated here, then spoke the next words carefully, "along with all the documents you need."

"Yes," I said. "The documents. I have them all."

"Excellent." I heard the excitement rise in his voice. "We're near Cathedral Square, on the corner of Gediminas and Tortoriu Streets. You can't miss us."

Cathedral Square? That would put me at the heart of the Baltic Way demonstration. For more than a year, Sąjūdis and all the other political groups had been holding rallies there regularly. Half the state security forces were likely to be in Cathedral Square tomorrow.

"Um, are you certain that's, um, the most convenient time?" I asked, hearing the sound of my own voice rise an octave as I spoke. "For you, I mean?"

But the line was dead. I considered asking the ugly girl for another coin, but her queue was long, and I suspected my call would not be answered. What was more, I needed to get out of there quickly before the girl or anyone else took any more notice of me.

The morning of August 23, 1989, dawned much like any other

summer day in Vilnius: foggy, with a refreshing chill in the air. The sounds of people talking behind their wide open windows woke me. Curtains on my own windows still closed against prying eyes, I took down the sweater and unfolded the papers from it.

I'd lain awake in my bed much of the night before, debating what I would do when morning came. The less I knew, the more I could deny. Perhaps I didn't want to see some of the names in those papers.

I was only a painter. I painted what I was told to paint. I saw what they wanted me to see and put it onto canvas. Perhaps the future of Lithuania should be decided by minds wiser than mine.

Then again, I am as curious as the next man, and when a man loses his curiosity, he may as well be dead. In the end, I decided this: If I was going to risk appearing in the human chain, risk being caught delivering papers to people likely known to the KGB as enemies of the state, then I had a right to know what was in them. So I sat on the edge of my bed in my underwear and placed the stack of papers on my naked knees and began to flip through them slowly.

The documents were both more and less than what I'd expected after my first hurried glance through them at the chicken coop. For the most part, they were ugly bureaucratic forms, in Lithuanian, Russian and German. Many of the papers were dry and brittle, the pages yellowed with age. Something had long ago spilled then dried in the lower right hand corner, and I had to be careful not to tear the pages as I separated them.

My Russian is as fluent as anyone educated in Soviet Lithuanian schools, my German passable; Lithuanian is of course my mother tongue. Some of the many different handwritings on the documents were spindly and old-fashioned, as befit the forty- and fifty-year-old papers. Others were much more recent.

Throughout its benighted history, Lithuania has been a pawn toyed with by much larger powers. During World War II, Hitler and

Stalin signed the Molotov-Ribbentrop Non-Aggression Pact, secretly dividing up East Central Europe between themselves rather than fight over it. In August of 1939, Lithuania had gone to the Germans. By September, Germany had swapped out most of Lithuania in order to get a large chunk of Poland. By early 1941, the last of Lithuania was formally incorporated into our great and beloved Union of Soviet Socialist Republics. If Hitler had simply decided to honor that pact, he might not have had to fight the Russians all the way to Stalingrad. When he'd been defeated once and for all, the Allies had tacitly decided to honor the pact Hitler had tossed aside, and left us to the Soviets.

The papers in my hands held the names and dates of smaller, though no less profound, betrayals. I read through lists of prisoners, dates of imprisonment, age, sex, the crimes of which they had been accused. For the information that didn't have fill-in-the-blanks or check boxes, there were large spaces for detailed notes. In these, too, were names the Lithuanian Communist Party would not want seen by the public. There were other papers summarizing reports from Lithuanian spies, agents, double agents and triple agents of both the Soviets and the Nazis.

So it came to pass that I learned how a great Lithuanian hero of our own small, Baltic-sized resistance against the Nazis had been executed by the Soviets in 1945, just before Germany surrendered, with the approval of officials in Berlin. The myth we'd grown up with was that he'd been killed while taking one of the last surviving groups of Lithuanian Jews to safety in Sweden.

I learned that the heads of three of our ministries today and a navy general had been spies with the same Gestapo handler. A well-known Lithuanian industrialist who'd fled the country just as the war was winding down had been marked for execution, when he'd been discovered to have been a double agent actually working under orders from the Soviet NKVD. The industrialist was known to have settled in Uruguay or Ecuador, or some other jungle nation. One newer paper contained a list of Lithuanians who had left the country and where they were now living in America, in cities like Cleveland, Los Angeles, Chicago, New York and Philadelphia.

Some of our best-known open secrets were in there too. A certain Lithuanian of German descent who was a member of the Lithuanian Soviet *nomenklatura* and who'd long and loudly declared his home to be a village near Kaunas. Or Kauen in his native German, as he sometimes called it. No one believed him, of course. As head of several of the largest state-owned factories in the Lithuanian SSR, he made a show of semi-hiding his favors to his so-called home village. Favors that were meant to be seen, in order to bolster his claim, as much as they were meant to buy off the support of the local villagers. There wasn't a man or woman in Lithuania who didn't know his true lineage, dating back to the German aristocracy. The documents in my hand merely provided details on how the Soviets had begun whitewashing his history as early as 1939.

Some of the surprises in these papers took my breath away. Others told me things many knew to be true. Still others confirmed what I might have known if I'd bothered to put two and two together long before. After a while, I might not have been startled to see my own father's name, which was impossible.

Now I knew why Antanas wanted these papers so badly. And I knew what Natalie had died for. But could these papers bring down the government? It seemed improbable. Still, what I had just seen had to be shown to the world. Even if no one else cared, every Lithuanian had the right to know.

I tapped the papers together against the tops of my sweaty knees, returned them to the envelope, and dressed for a revolution.

True revolutionaries dress to blend in. Not like your occupy this-or-that protests these days, where young people attire themselves in all manner of filthy jeans and obscene t-shirts hoisting signs above their heads, parading around dressed in giant puppet costumes. That is political theater, not revolution. Trust me, your government knows the difference, and they are not impressed by childish playacting.

The crowds in and around Cathedral Square were larger than I'd imagined. What we had in Cathedral Square that day was simple proof to the powers that be, that remarkable numbers of ordinary men and women were willing to walk away from home and work, to be seen in public. How was it possible so many people knew about the human chain?

Then again, how many in the crowd were police, informants, intelligence, spies?

Families in the crowd were dressed in a mix of formality, women in skirts and blouses, men in suit jackets and matching trousers. They dressed their younger children much the same. Teenagers, though, wore the latest western fashions: blue jeans and black vinyl jackets, sleeves pulled up to their elbows, collars turned up. The teenage girls and some of the boys wore their hair teased up, held in place with clips and rubber bands. Old ladies wrapped their heads in kerchiefs. Here and there stood groups of women and men dressed in traditional Lithuanian clothes with puffed peasant sleeves and round white hats with folk stitching around the sides. From time to time these groups would break into traditional Lithuanian folk songs. When they did, the crowds around them joined in.

How many in this crowd were *druzhenniki*? How many KGB provocateurs? The Cathedral was ringed by uniformed militia, but they stood back watching and did not interfere with the demonstration.

For the first time I wondered—how many of those soldiers

would have preferred to join in?

Natalie's documents were in a small leatherette valise that I gripped tightly in my right hand as I pushed my way through the throng. I'd stuffed several more envelopes full of papers into the bag to camouflage the important ones, sandwiched between two small, unframed oil paintings to fill the case. If I was stopped in the streets and searched by the militia, they might not notice the truly important papers amidst all the detritus.

I'd taken time over the selection of the paintings. I am, after all, an artist, not a spy. If I were caught, I wanted to give the right message. At the same time, part of me wanted to be able to say I'd thumbed my nose at the authorities. One painting showed a bucolic rural Lithuanian scene, happy family in the foreground with its cow. The heroic heartland, good, strong people surrounded by rolling fields, raising their dairy cattle for the greater good. I'd spent several days in a village in the north, painting scenes, dining with the families, getting a taste of the strong, adept local girls. The irony was that the family who'd modeled for this painting had lost several members in the Stalinist deportations of the 1940s.

For the second painting I dropped into the valise, I'd opted for a bit of Soviet Lithuanian realism—a close-up of eager workers in caps and kerchiefs, Lithuanian flag fluttering in the breeze, looking off into a quintessentially bright communist future. If I could get these papers to the right hands and if the circumstances played themselves out the way Natalie had hoped, this kind of scene and perhaps the art that went with it would soon be history.

The farther I got into the square, the more dense the crowd grew. Soon I was shoving my way through with both arms outstretched. For one frightening moment, my valise caught against someone. I pushed forward but I could not tug the bag loose from behind me. I yanked, I jerked. Mostly I held on tight with my sweaty right hand.

Finally, someone shouted and moved, freeing me with a jolt.

I hugged it to my chest, checking the two metal latches on top. They were closed, seemingly undamaged. I took a deep breath and plunged further into the melee.

As I approached the corner where the travel agent had directed me, someone shouted my name. I looked up and all about the crowd. A hand flew into the air. I followed the arm down until I saw Indre standing by the doorway of an office. I began shoving my way through the crowd toward her.

Suddenly, I caught a glimpse of a man's familiar face to my left. Familiar, but not well known to me. Someone who put me on edge. He wasn't a friend. Nor a cuckolded husband. I didn't recognize him from the university nor from the arts community. I continued pushing toward Indre. The familiar man turned away and melted into the crowd.

Perhaps I'd been wrong. Perhaps he only looked familiar. Perhaps my mind was playing tricks on me, trying to find something familiar in this setting that was so strange: an independence demonstration, me standing stupidly with a valise full of documents that could bring down a government.

Then, in a flash, the man's name was on my lips. Pablo. That familiar face belonged to the young man with his hair in his eyes. The young man I'd met in the park across from the house of General Degutis. I stopped abruptly, made myself as tall as I could and scanned the crowd rapidly. Pablo was gone.

But I was close now, to Indre and to the shop where Antanas was waiting for the papers. Even if seeing Pablo was not a coincidence— and a lifetime in a Soviet country teaches you there are no such things as coincidences—I still had no choice. I continued to press on to meet Indre. When I was just beside her, I leaned in to speak to her. Even though I was close, I still had to shout to make myself heard over the sounds of the crowd.

"What are you doing here?"

"What are you doing here?" she shouted back.

"I found them," I said, then looked down at the valise.

Indre's eyes followed mine. When she looked up again, she was smiling, and there were tears in her eyes. "I didn't think you would do it."

To my surprise, tears plucked at my eyes too. I smiled back at her. "Natalie," I said. I wanted to say more, but couldn't speak for the lump in my throat.

The noise of the crowd suddenly rose several decibels. I was shoved from behind, hard. From where I stood, I couldn't see the cause of it. I put my arm around Indre protectively and spoke directly into her ear. "Let's get this to our friend." My lips brushed against her ear as I spoke. She didn't pull away.

Indre nodded. We began pushing our way toward the shop door at the corner.

I tried to keep one arm around her, but it was too hard to get ourselves through the crowd side by side. "Hold onto me," I said. I would clear the way for her. I wrapped my arms around the valise and pushed forward with my chest and shoulders. I could feel Indre's fists against my back as she gripped my jacket.

We were nearly at the shop door when I felt Indre let go. My jacket suddenly went slack against my chest. I quickly turned back. The crowd was mysteriously melting away behind me. Someone screamed and pointed down at the sidewalk. Indre had crumpled to the ground.

Below her, a pool of blood was beginning to form.

For a moment, I was frozen, staring at her, watching the red pool grow larger and larger. Part of me wanted to kneel beside her and help her. Another part wanted to fling the valise aside and run.

Another part needed to know what had happened. I looked around, scanning the faces of the crowd that surrounded Indre. Nearly all of them were staring down at her lifeless body. Then I saw him almost directly across from me.

Pablo. He wasn't looking down at Indre. He was staring right at me and grinning. His hands were stuffed into the pockets of his leather jacket.

Someone grabbed me from behind and began pulling me backward. I jerked away.

"Come on," a man's voice said. "We've got to get out of here."

It was Antanas.

"But Indre...."

He grabbed my shoulders and yanked me, hard.

I resisted. "The young man over there, in the leather jacket. Longish black hair. Who is he?"

Antanas and I looked across the way together. Pablo was trying to work his way toward me, but the thick crowd slowed him.

"Forget him. At least with the KGB there is a chance of surviving prison," Antanas said. "We must go now!"

This time when he shoved me, I went with him. We made our way to a shop, got the door open just wide enough to slip inside.

It was dark inside, and cool like a cave. The lights were out, and Antanas made no effort to turn them on. Enough daylight seeped in through cracks in the curtains that I could see it was a household goods shop. In the dark, the nearly empty shelves hovered as menacing shadows.

Two more men appeared from the back. "You have it?" one of them asked me.

I looked to Antanas.

"These are my colleagues in the movement, Justas and Stasys," he said.

It dawned on me that I did not know Antanas at all. Kurt may have been an American, but I had no proof he was a spy. I had no proof Antanas was who he'd said he was. I felt the trap closing in.

"Did you know Natalie?" I asked the two men.

Both men nodded. "It is a terrible loss," one of them said, either Justas or Stasys.

I had come this far, and Indre was dead now too. The papers were in my hands. If I walked out the door now, Pablo would find me.

I placed the valise on the counter and opened it. Now I wished I hadn't stuffed it full of paintings and papers that would so obviously connect it to me. But it was too late for regrets.

I found the right envelope and took it from the valise. The three men huddled together as Antanas opened it and flipped through the papers.

"Yes, this is it," the other man said, either Justas or Stasys.

Antanas turned to me. "You've done well. For Natalie and for your country."

To my surprise, there were tears streaming down my cheeks.

One of the other men clapped me on the back in a friendly way. "This deserves a toast," he said, "but we have nothing here. When Lithuania is free, we will drink together."

"The man in the leather coat," I said. "He calls himself Pablo. I think he killed Indre."

"Most likely so," Antanas said.

"Who is he?"

"There is a new class of men on the ascendancy. Men with money. Some of them come from the military, some from high up in government, some from the state industries. Some are ordinary criminals hardened by their time in the Kolyma camps. They work entirely outside the law. *Glasnost* and *perestroika* are making them very wealthy. They have begun to hire their own independent enforcers."

"He is a gangster? Like Al Capone?" I asked. The gangster was a legend, even in Lithuania. We learned about him as the epitome of what was wrong with American capitalism.

"Yes, well, no. These new-style men don't have to rob banks. They buy and sell on markets you don't even know exist."

Markets. In my mind I imagined an old village woman in a kerchief hawking her wares in the streets. This, I knew, was not what Antanas meant.

A scraping sound at the door caught my ears. They must have heard it too, because we all turned toward the sound simultaneously. Antanas stuffed Natalie's papers into a pocket inside his jacket.

The scraping became a pounding. The shop door shook on its hinges.

"This way," Antanas said. I followed him into the back of the shop. He flung open the back door and looked in both directions. Justas and Stasys stepped through the door next.

There was a crash behind me and I turned in time to see Pablo and two other young men shoving glass into the shop from the broken front window.

"Come on!" Antanas shouted. One of the other men grabbed me by the arm and pulled me out of the shop and into the alley.

Antanas was already headed down the alley, the three of us following quickly behind.

"You won't get very far!" Pablo shouted from behind us. His voice sounded frighteningly close on our heels.

Justas—or was it Stasys?—grabbed my arm and fairly pulled me along as we took a left, a right then another right. As we ran and stumbled through the alleys, I could hear the distant sound of the crowd in the square. The sound of thousands of voices, talking, singing, shouting, laughing.

The thuds of Pablo's boots and those of his colleagues stayed close behind us. We kept running away from the square and toward, well, I didn't know what or where.

Where were they leading me? Into safety, I'd assumed all along. But what place in Vilnius, in all the Baltics, was safe on a day like this?

I must have slowed, because one of the men ahead of me turned back and shouted, "Don't give up now! We're almost there."

Where was "there?" ·

We took a quick left. Antanas stopped at a metal ladder and leapt up it, taking three rungs at a time. Where it had come from, and where we even were, I didn't know. At the top, Antanas disappeared over the wall. One of the men stood by the ladder and shoved me up it while the other grabbed the valise from my hands and hurled it up over the wall.

When I was over the wall I saw where it had landed. We were on top of a shed behind a single family home. Justas and Stasys lifted the ladder and pushed it up. I helped Antanas lift it up and over the wall we'd just scaled. We lay it flat on the roof. Evidently, the two other men weren't coming with us.

Footsteps approached up the alley. Justas and Stasys took off running. Antanas slapped my back and shoved me flat onto the shed roof. It was just slightly lower than the height of the wall. By lying flat and still, we would not be visible from the alley. I hoped.

From where I lay flat on my stomach, valise clenched to my chest, I saw it all. One of the men slipped on a pile of dog shit and fell to his knee. He was up again quickly, but Pablo was already on him, knife poised in his fist.

"Ah, no, Justas," Antanas muttered beside me and shook his head ever so gently.

Stasys didn't look back, escaping down the alley at top speed. Pablo slammed the knife into Justas's back once, driving him to his knees with the force of his blow. A second thrust with the knife, then a third. Justas collapsed on the smooth, ancient paving stones that had lined Vilnius's alleys for centuries. Pablo kicked him twice for good measure, wiped blood from the blade onto Justas's pants, and took off running. I could hear Stasys' footsteps in the distance. I was sure Pablo could too.

Antanas and I lay there, still and silent, as the sound of footsteps disappeared down the alley. When I couldn't hear them any longer, I pressed my hands beneath me to get up. But Antanas held me down with a strong arm on my back.

"Listen," he said.

I did. The voices in Cathedral Square had changed. The shouts, the laughter, all the little conversations had come together. The people of Vilnius, my people, were speaking with one voice now, and they were singing our new, modern rock anthem to freedom, *Bunda jau Baltija.*

> "*Three sisters wake up from sleep,*
> *Come to stand for themselves.*
> *The Baltics are waking up, the Baltics are waking up.*
> *Lithuania, Latvia, Estonia!*"

There on the roof of an old shed in a Vilnius alley, Antanas and I lay still, transfixed by the beautiful sound of their voices carried by the wind through the streets, along the alleyways, across my beloved city. They were waking up and so was I, to the sound of our Baltic future.

In that moment, I felt my heart break for Natalie. She should be there with me. Instead of me. This was what she had lived and died for. It should be her on this roof, on this day, in this hour of hope, not me.

EIGHT

HOPE FOR THE FUTURE, YES, but a distant one. For now, Antanas and I had to survive that day and the next, and the ones that would follow close upon them.

We lay flat on our bellies atop that shed for hours, until the shape of the rusty corrugated metal was imprinted on my liver and spleen. The sun was warm on my back, and the distant sounds of singing and cheers were like lullabies ebbing and flowing in the wind. I dozed off, only to be awakened by the sound of running feet and breaking glass. Antanas tensed beside me. We watched a group of young men race up the alley, laughing and singing songs of the revolution in drunken splendor. When they came upon Justas's body, they laughed more loudly and shouted at him to "Get up you drunken fool!"

One of the boys kicked at Justas. Another poured vodka over him. A third squatted down beside him and finally noticed the blood pooling beneath him. He jerked back upright and shouted, "He's dead!"

They didn't need a second warning. They sprinted down the alley in silence, suddenly sobered by the kind of reality their Soviet Lithuanian upbringing had not prepared them for very well.

When the boys were out of earshot I reached for the pack of cigarettes in my jacket pocket, but Antanas stopped me with a warning hand that shook with nicotine withdrawal.

It was summer and night didn't fall until after eight in Vilnius. We listened as the demonstration hit its crescendo a little after seven. Then people began to disperse, chatting, laughing, and of course singing. As dusk became night and the temperature dropped, Antanas and I edged closer to each other for warmth. Otherwise, we remained still. We listened as the sounds changed from celebration to something more ominous and familiar—soldiers shouting orders and clearing streets.

It was nearly midnight when my bladder finally couldn't take it any more. I leaned into Antanas's ear and told him as much. He nodded and gestured for me to lift the ladder with him. We lowered it to alley floor. It clattered slightly against a pile of rocks. Antanas and I went still for several minutes. When we heard no reaction or response, Antanas gestured for me to climb down.

I stood, frozen, over the body of a man who'd saved my life. Antanas joined me and crossed himself, muttering something under his breath. I shared the moment with him, though in truth I was not there at all. He may have been paying his respects to a man called Justas, but that was not what I was looking at. I saw Indre and Natalie, and they deserved so much more than sanctimonious gestures.

We carried the ladder around the corner with us, laying it on its side amidst a pile of tree branches. Antanas rearranged the branches while I pissed against the opposite wall. When he took his turn against the wall, I stared at the ladder in its place, looked nervously up and down the alley. It was too dark to know if it was adequately camouflaged, and we didn't have time for certainties.

I followed Antanas through the alleys. We slipped into a quiet side street unnoticed. We were several blocks away walking through the open streets when Antanas came to a stop and growled in a low voice, "How about one of those cigarettes?" I shook two out of the pack, handed him one. We lit them both on a single match and inhaled the pungent smoke with gusto. It had been many hours since my last cigarette.

He seemed to be using the moment for reconnaissance, scanning the eerily empty streets. We stood, smoking, trying to look like ordinary Vilniusites going about our ordinary business. But after such an extraordinary day, would anything look ordinary?

"You must leave Lithuania," Antanas said quietly. "If Pablo can't find you and take care of you himself, he'll report you to the authorities. If they connect you to Kurt, you're as good as dead."

I was suddenly overcome with exhaustion. I was tired of dead bodies and I didn't want to be part of this fight any longer. "You have the papers. This isn't my problem." I had done everything I could.

"You are part of the movement now, and I am responsible. We have to get you to safety."

"I really don't care what happens now."

Antanas frowned. "You may not care, but we care about what you know, and you know things that could hurt the movement. You wouldn't last long under KGB questioning."

Natalie and Indre had given their lives to this fight, and now, it seemed, I was going to have to as well. Only they would have the distinct advantage of being dead, while I would have to live on.

"You know the Užupis?"

"Of course," I said.

"Find a cheap flop. Every day between two and three in the afternoon, go to one of the cafeterias in Užupis and wait. There aren't many. Someone will meet you. Do you have money?"

I considered the cost of a cheap room and vodka. "Enough for a week, eight days at most."

"Don't worry. We will have you well out of Lithuania by then."

"I could go to Kaunas." The second city of Lithuania.

"It's not far enough. We have to get you out of the country. Germany, perhaps, or Sweden. I'll have to see what I can do."

A pair of militiamen turned the corner and spotted us. Antanas stamped his feet and stared at the ground. "*Po simts geguciu,*" he muttered. He took a flask I hadn't noticed before from his jacket pocket, took a long drink and handed it to me. I drank.

Suddenly Antanas laughed a little too loudly, grabbed the flask from me and stumbled a bit. I didn't need further instruction. We were to act drunk. I laughed with him.

"Hey, you!" the militiamen shouted as they closed in. "Stop right there!"

"If they look in the…" Antanas began, then stopped abruptly to look me up and down. "Where is your valise?"

I held my hands out in front of me, surprised to see that they held nothing more than a cigarette that I had smoked down to the filter. I threw it on the ground and squashed it beneath my foot.

"I… I must have left it on the shed." The militiamen were close. I reached for the flask, hoping my face didn't give away my sudden terror.

Antanas kept up with our street theater and laughed, but in the dim streetlight I could see fear in his eyes.

"Natalie's documents?" I whispered, holding my eyes steady on his so I wouldn't look at the place in his jacket where I'd seen him secret them hours ago, back in the shop.

"Safe. I left them at a dead drop three blocks back. But the valise…." He shook his head.

"Your identity papers!" a militiaman shouted. They were upon us.

Antanas stumbled a little against me as he reached for his papers. I giggled like a silly drunk and patted my pockets.

"You two have a little too much fun in the demonstration today?"

My identification papers were mine, and I was Martynas Kudirka, proud painter of the Soviet Republic of Realism. I didn't know what Antanas's papers would show and didn't want to know. He handed them over with a confidence that said he could rely on them to keep him out of suspicion. Was "Antanas" even his real name?

One of the militiamen glared at us while the other took his time looking over our documents. First mine, then Antanas's.

"What do you think?" the militiaman holding our papers said to the other. "Should we let them go, or take them to the Department of Percussion Instruments and Solo Singing?"

Take us in to be questioned by KGB, in other words.

The other militiaman grunted, never taking his eyes off us.

"Ungrateful bastards," the talkative one continued. "The Lithuanian state feeds you and clothes you and provides for all your needs. You thank them by blocking traffic to hold hands with filthy Estonians and Latvians."

Another grunt.

"You intellectuals make me sick." He looked down and spat on my shoes.

For that, the other militiaman gave him a short bark of a laugh.

My stomach churned with fear. These militiamen could drop us into the pit of hell that was KGB custody. The valise full of my documents and paintings would be discovered soon enough. They would find a way to connect me to the independence movement, to Kurt, then they would blame me for Natalie's death. I turned to get a sidelong look at Antanas, who swayed a little on his feet, but otherwise looked calm and cool.

And then, to my surprise, I puked. There wasn't much to come up, mostly stomach acids and spit.

"Bloody hell!" the talkative militiaman said, jumping back.

The other raised his rifle and shoved me with the butt of it, hard, saying, simply, "Drunks."

"Sorry," I said, wiping a string of saliva from my chin with the back of my hand. I smiled a little, hoping it made me look stupid.

The militiaman handed our identity papers back to Antanas. "Get your friend out of here before we shoot him," he said.

Antanas clapped an arm around my shoulder and dragged me away. The two militiamen stood there, cursing and watching us as we made our way down the street.

I ran out of money after five days. On the seventh day, the old woman who ran the Užupis flophouse where I had been sleeping decided she had given me a free ride for long enough and threw me out into the streets. That night I slept in a doorway for the first time in my life.

I'd scoured the Užupis district and discovered three cafeterias. I took turns each day to visit one of them between two and three in the afternoon. Just to be sure, I always arrived long before two and left long after three. No one came for me.

I spent the eighth day on a bench in the Bernardine Cemetery, considering my options. Go home. Find friends. Search for Antanas. A little before one o'clock, I left the cemetery bench and made my way to one of the cafeterias. I gathered up enough small coins from my pockets to buy the smallest, meanest bottle of vodka in the shop. I nursed it for three hours before being rousted from my chair. No one came to take me away. That night I found my doorway and slept there again.

The ninth day of waiting for my knight in shining armor to come save me was cold and drizzly. I found a bench at a small park where I sat for hours with the collar of my jacket turned up. At one in the afternoon I made my way to a different cafeteria. This time I had no small coins left, so I charmed a bottle of vodka and a plate of bread and pickles off the homely girl at the till. She responded to me with a wary, pitying look in her eye, not the wanton look of curiosity I was usually able to elicit from her type. Sitting down at a table in the corner, I caught a glimpse of my reflection in the window and understood. I'd aged a hundred years since my beautiful Natalie had been killed. My cheeks were sunken, my hair thick with grease. The narrow runnels of gray I remembered had expanded to wide, mottled patches. I looked down at the hands that gripped my bottle and glass. The crescents of dirt under my untrimmed nails revolted me.

At half past four I finished the bottle and finally swallowed the cold, bitter truth with it. No one from the independence movement was coming to help me escape from Lithuania. Lithuania's revolution lived on, but mine was dead. I was on my own.

In the toilet behind the cafeteria I took off my shirt and washed the top layer of grime from my upper body, then scrubbed under my nails with a loose screw I pried from the wall. I raked my hands through my hair to comb it in place as best I could. I was barely presentable, so I held my head high to compensate as I walked across the city, lacking even the fare for the trolleybus.

I found myself mimicking Antanas and Kurt as I walked through the streets of my beloved city, peering around corners and backtracking across my own steps through cobbled streets, in fear for my safety. Like an old lover one returns to after experiences with other women, Vilnius seemed like a whole new city to me. It was smaller somehow, its familiar nooks and crannies now alien and peculiar. I didn't want her, yet I feared her rejection.

I stood in shadows across from the bakery for half an hour, watching shoppers pass in the front door and out again. Something was wrong.

Each one of them left without any evidence of a purchase. As dusk began to fall I stepped quickly across the street and slipped inside.

"There is no bread today," the baker Adolfas shouted without looking to see who'd entered. The shelves were empty, and the shop smelled stale.

"Where is Žemyna?" I said.

He whipped around, an angry scowl on his face. When he saw me, his look softened. "Oh, it's you." The baker shook his head sadly.

"What has happened?" Even the cloud of flour that usually hung in the air was gone.

"They've taken her."

This really threw me off my stride. "Who?" I asked. "Žemyna?" It wasn't possible. She wasn't political.

Adolfas simply shook his head again. "It's beginning to look like 1948 all over again. They simply appear and take people away."

"Oh, god, no."

"I told Žemyna not to go to the human chain, but the young can be so full of hope. Even in Soviet Lithuania."

"You know for certain she was arrested, or has she just disappeared?"

"I saw it with my own eyes. Žemyna came to work the day after the human chain, even though we had no flour. She kept coming back even though there was no bread to be baked," Adolfas said. "Three days later they came looking for her by name. They spoke Russian."

We stared at each other, sharing a moment of silent bitterness for all things Russian.

I had to go. "If you see her, tell her I came for her," I said, though none of it was true. I hadn't come to help her, but for her to help me. And I knew the baker would never see Žemyna again.

"If I see her," the baker echoed. "I don't know your name but I know who you are. Let us leave it at that."

I nodded and reached for the front door.

"Be careful," he said.

"I know."

It was fully dark now, and I took each block one dark doorway at a time on my way to my apartment. Where else could I go? I needed a shower, a shave, a decent night's sleep and clean clothes. I needed a quiet place where I could think clearly. I had money hidden away. Not much, but enough to get me into the countryside. With a little luck, I might be able to make the Polish frontier.

A dark blue Lada passed me as I turned the corner onto Erfurto Street, only a block from my apartment building. I looked away from the car to keep my face out of view. When I looked back, the Lada was braking for a stop sign up ahead. The passenger door opened and a man climbed out. Instinctively, I stepped into a doorway. I was becoming an aficionado of doorways, and I didn't like this one. Too shallow, but it would have to do. With a squeal of tires the Lada sped away, and I looked down the sidewalk to see Pablo staring into the upper windows of my apartment building.

I was instantly bathed in cold, clammy sweat. It took every ounce of will in my body not to retch.

I grabbed the door handle behind me and turned it as quietly as I could, pulling the door open as I did.

I found myself in a shoe store, at least that's what it should have been, but the shelves were nearly bare. There was no one to be seen. One bare light bulb hung from the ceiling.

I walked through the store and into the storeroom in back where two women sat side by side next to a crate, staring at me, fear in their eyes.

One of the women—she seemed to be the older of the two—shoved her chin forward. "Go away. We have nothing for sale."

As she did, the other woman slipped something in her left hand behind her back. I saw the transistor radio before she could hide it.

"Romas?" I asked, pointing to where she was hiding the radio from me.

I didn't have to say a last name. Her face went red, and she placed the transistor on the crate.

"Turn it on," I said. Maybe he would tell us something so I would know what to do or where to go now. Where were the political dissidents gathering? Where were their safe houses? Who should I look for, or what? Names? Clothing? Secret handshakes?

Where was Antanas and why hadn't he come for me?

The shoe clerk's hands shook as she twisted the knob. Reception was scratchy and the volume had to be kept low, so I squatted down beside the women. The three of us leaned in close to listen.

Sakadolskis was telling stories from people all across the Baltic states who'd participated in the human chain. Don't be fooled by news accounts about the Baltic Way, he told us. When the Central Committee of the Communist Party puts out statements to be read on the evening news across all the Soviet republics, you know you have achieved something great. They may warn against nationalist, extremist groups and call the demonstration "nationalist hysteria," but the truth was that two million people across Lithuania, Estonia and Latvia had joined hands together in the Baltic Way.

Two million people. Even the Soviet news agency had admitted to the presence of half a million of us in Lithuania alone. The Western press said we had been twice that many. It was hard to imagine. I listened as Sakadolskis announced there had been five thousand of us in Cathedral Square. Including Indre, Pablo and me. He told us about solidarity protests in cities from West Berlin to Washington, DC. There was no mention of anyone dying in Cathedral Square. The Party was covering up Indre's murder.

There was a shout in the street, and the clerk snapped off the radio. We stared in the direction of the door, but no one entered. Sakadolskis was encouraging us to stay strong, to keep up the fight.

We had been strong that day. I had proven myself to be something more than I'd thought myself to be. But now I was sleeping on the streets, on the run from the state, from Pablo, and perhaps from the Americans too. My strength was fading fast.

"You should lock your front door," I said. Much as I wanted to, I couldn't stay in this shop any longer.

"They've told us to keep normal hours, even though we have nothing to sell," the younger shop woman said.

"Locked would look suspicious," the older one added.

"Do you have a back door, by any chance?" I asked. The two women shook their heads.

I went to the front door and pulled it open, just a crack. Enough to see Pablo look at his watch, shake his shoulders inside his jacket and begin walking down the street toward me. I shut the door and listened as he passed. Once his footsteps had disappeared into the distance, I opened the door again, saw no one, and stepped out quickly. I stayed in shadows as I walked down the street in the opposite direction.

I made it back to Užupis district a little after midnight. Somehow in my mind it was home base, a safe place. Which was of course ridiculous. But at least it was not a place I was known to frequent. Pablo was still looking for me at my old home. I hoped the security services would take the same approach.

For my third night on the street I found a row of thick shrubs behind an abandoned factory. I curled up into the fetal position and considered my meager options. I needed someone political enough to have connections, but not so political they would be watched. But I remembered Žemyna, and wondered if there was such a thing as apolitical now. All those years I had thought of myself as apolitical. Now I had to wonder, had apolitical ever existed in Soviet Lithuania?

Day ten after the human chain I awoke late in the morning, surprised to find myself still huddled in the dirt. My bones ached, and my stomach gurgled uncomfortably.

I made my way into the daily life of Vilnius, but this wasn't like any morning I'd ever lived through before. My city, founded by a man with fourteenth century visions of an iron wolf on a hill, fought over for centuries by Poles, Germans, Russians and—oh, yes, let's not forget them—Lithuanians, perhaps it had seen a thousand days like this one. A day marked with uncertainty, fear and hope crackling in the air. People would not meet my eyes in the streets. Or they would smile wide, unnatural, un-Lithuanian smiles and nod as if in recognition. Who among them was Sąjūdis, who KGB? Who were *druzhenniki* and who were ordinary Lithuanian citizens hoping for a brighter future?

I wandered the streets of Užupis district slowly. My back ached and my empty belly demanded attention. When I stopped on one corner to consider whether to turn left or right or simply to keep moving forward, a man I did not know who was also waiting for traffic to clear handed me a cigarette and lit it. I narrowed my eyes and looked him up and down. He lit his own cigarette and lifted it to me in a mock salute, then continued on his way. I took a different direction rather than follow him.

As I walked, I went through a mental list of my friends and colleagues. Who would be willing to help me? Who could? Who would have the kinds of connections I needed to get out of the country in these parlous days? Who among them had already used up those connections and left the country themselves? Who would pretend to help, then sell me out for a chance at their own freedom?

Two in the afternoon found my feet carrying me back to one of the Užupis cafeterias. They had taken me there of their own volition, without my mind directing them. I had no money, and no energy for the effort it would take to charm the inevitable shopgirl out of a little of her wares. As I approached, men suddenly began pouring out of the shop, shouting as they came out into the open air. Some of them stumbled away in a drunken stupor. The crowd that remained curled itself into a fist and stood on the sidewalk shouting.

Soon enough, their shouts made everything clear. The shop had run out of vodka. The shortages were reaching a crisis if Soviets couldn't get their vodka. If a lack of bread will drive even the meekest of women into the street to protest, then vodka will do the same for men.

No doubt there would be a riot soon. Police would appear. Heads would be broken open at random. I turned to retrace my steps. I turned left at the next corner, crossed the street to take the next right. I was halfway down a quiet block when a hand grabbed my arm from behind. I shook it off and began walking more quickly.

"Martynas!" The hand took my arm once more. This time it held on firmly. I raised an elbow to fend off my attacker.

"Hey, Kudirka. Cut it out!" the man said, knocking my elbow away with a meaty forearm.

"I'm not Martynas Kudirka," I said, beginning to panic. "Go away!"

"Don't make a fuss," the man said, more quietly this time. He grabbed both my arms in his hands and turned me around to face him. Weakened by hunger and fear, I couldn't resist.

"I don't know who you think I am," I said. "Leave me alone." He was bigger and beefier than me, and at least fifteen years younger. He wore civilian clothes, but his hair had been cut to military precision.

"I am Gintaras. Gintaras Degutis."

He must have seen me flinch at that name, because he said, "No, it's okay."

"You killed my wife!"

It was his turn to look confused. "No," he said. "I didn't."

His confusion was real, and in that moment I realized I'd never believed the student whose paper was found in Natalie's hand had killed her. It was too ridiculous to be true, and too straightforward to happen in a Soviet state. "What do you want from me? I thought you had left for Poland."

"I did. My family is there. I returned for the revolution. This is Lithuania's hour."

Finally, the trap was snapping closed. I took a deep breath, then exhaled it loudly. My hands shook by my sides.

Gintaras leaned in close and lowered his voice. "I'm here to take you to safety. What you did for the movement is known."

At this, I felt my shoulders rise involuntarily. "Take me where?" I asked.

Gintaras shook his head. "Just come with me."

He began walking, but I didn't move. *Come with me.* Those words had sent a chill down my spine. When he noticed I wasn't following, he stopped.

"Why should I trust you?"

"Because you have no choice. You can't go home. Your malcontent artist friends have less to offer than you might hope. The KGB has taken your pretty little baker—who else might they have taken already? Pablo has realized you are not returning home, so he's going to start combing the rest of the city to find and kill you. If you don't die of starvation in the streets first."

So my life had come to this. I was a painter. I was known. And yet I was no one. I was like a helpless babe in the hands of this man who somehow knew everything about me.

I gestured with my chin for Gintaras to lead. I would follow.

NINE

IT TURNED OUT TO BE EASIER to hand myself over to another man's lead than I might have expected. Perhaps I was more truly Soviet than I had previously believed. Within myself I was exhausted, hungry and utterly without hope. An artist, I might wield brushstrokes, metaphor and irony against the more constrictive aspects of state control, but the past week had proven I clearly lacked the practical wits to get myself to safety when in mortal danger. In a half-blind, silent daze I followed Gintaras through the streets of my city.

We were on a narrow side street in the heart of Old Town when a beige Volga pulled up beside us and the passenger door flew open. I tensed my legs to run, but Gintaras grabbed my arm.

"Get in! Quickly."

I fairly hurtled into the car and Gintaras followed close behind. Before he'd even closed the door, we were moving.

The two men in the front seat did not speak, so I followed their lead. The four of us sat staring straight ahead. My heart thudded against my chest. If this was a mistake, then I was making it with every ounce of manhood I had left inside me. I thought of Natalie, Indre and Justas, all of whom had given themselves up to a brighter future for our country. I could do nothing less than what they had done. This car was taking me either to an end or a beginning. I would be in Russian custody soon enough, or safe somewhere that the Russians would not find me. Or dead enough that none of it would matter.

We were at the outskirts of the city pulling onto the highway when to my surprise I realized the car was heading into the sunset.

"We're going west," I said, finally breaking the silence. Not south to Poland, or north to Latvia.

The driver glanced into the mirror as the passenger beside him said, "Yes."

They're taking me to Kaunas, I thought. There were worse places in the world to be exiled. The second largest city in Lithuania, it was known for its arts and universities. The cultural heartland of our nation, and a hotbed of independence activities and demonstrations. A man like me wouldn't stand out so much. Away from the machinery of the state in the capitol, I would be safer.

Soon enough we were arriving at the edge of the city.

But rather than going into the heart of the city, our driver followed a road that led us around the outskirts. We were on the open road again, still heading west.

"You're not taking me to Kaunas?" I asked.

"Klaipeda," Gintaras said. Lithuania's largest port city, on the Baltic Sea.

He must have seen the surprise on my face, because he continued, "There is a ship for Gotland departing in the early hours tomorrow. You will be on that ship."

I could hardly believe my ears. "Sweden?" Gotland was an island of Western territory in the midst of the Baltic Sea, barely two hundred and fifty kilometers away by distance. A lifetime away in politics.

"That's enough for now," the driver said.

Neither Gintaras nor I said another word the rest of the drive.

Four hours later we were alone, seated on ramshackle wooden chairs in the basement of an old abandoned church near the Port of Klaipeda.

It had been dark by the time the two men in the car had dropped us off in front of a hotel and had driven away. Neither of them had spoken again. Rather than walk into the hotel, Gintaras and I had walked in a circular fashion around five city blocks. We'd crept through the churchyard and entered through a small door in back of the church.

I leaned back in my chair to survey the small space. It was empty other than three chairs, a small table and a stack of blankets in the corner. The church we'd passed through had been strewn with the detritus of a dying faith—splintered pews, tarnished censers and crosses—but this room was clean, no dust or cobwebs. Nor was there anything extra or unnecessary.

Gintaras perched on the edge of his chair, watching me. "We are safe here, for now."

"This is a safe house," I said. As familiar as the phrase was in my mind, it felt awkward and unfamiliar on my tongue. I had become the kind of person who needed a "safe house."

Gintaras gestured to the stack of blankets in the corner. "You should get some rest now. I'll wake you when it's time to leave."

"I don't suppose there's a shower," I said.

Gintaras shook his head. "The water was cut off to this building long ago."

I would like to say I was enough of a man to argue with Gintaras.

I want to report that I sat up with him all night talking strategy and politics until the signal came that it was time for us to leave. That I didn't require a nanny or caretaker or watchman.

Instead, I will tell the truth. With my guardian angel watching over me in my cocoon of safety, I stripped down to my briefs, wrapped myself up in blankets and slept like a baby.

When Gintaras shook me awake it was still dark. Disoriented, I started to ask him to put on the light, but he placed a finger on my lips to tell me to keep quiet. I did not like having a man's hands on my face, and I shook myself away violently. I slipped back into my filthy pants and shirt while Gintaras stood by the door, watching through the slight crack he'd opened. The only sound in the room was the rustle of fabric as I changed clothes. Once I was dressed he opened the door and motioned for me to follow.

Gintaras picked his way down the hall swiftly. I followed, a little more slowly. When I tripped over something bulky in the dark and muttered a curse, Gintaras froze.

"Shhh," he whispered softly.

We slipped out the back door we'd entered through. I kept close to Gintaras as we walked through the tumbledown churchyard, our pathway lit by a half-moon hanging low in the sky. The air was moist, and the salty smell of the sea burned my nostrils.

Both of us must have seen the man pass under the street light at the corner at the same time, because we froze in our steps simultaneously. It was an hour when only drunks or militiamen would have a plausible reason to be out in the streets, and this man was too sure-footed and stealthy for either. But I knew even more. I had seen his profile clearly. I gripped Gintaras's arm tightly.

"Pablo," I whispered.

In the same moment, Gintaras flung out his arm to keep me from moving forward. We stood, immobilized, watching Pablo. He, too, had stopped in mid-stride. I barely breathed, watching him turn to look in our direction.

Gintaras squatted down without making a sound. I did the same. Pablo scanned the churchyard methodically. In the motion of his head I could see him marking it out in a grid. I almost felt his eyes upon us as he passed over the section containing Gintaras and myself.

How Pablo saw the back door to the church, I don't know. Perhaps he'd already known it was there. He squinted and leaned in to get a better look. My knees turned to jelly beneath me, and my breath came shallow and fast. Gintaras grabbed my arm.

Pablo stepped into the churchyard, heading straight for the back door. His feet made so little noise as he jogged across the yard that I might have taken him for an American Indian in moccasins. He paused at the door long enough to pull a knife from its holster under his jacket. He pulled the door open and slipped inside.

The moment the door shut behind Pablo, Gintaras grabbed my arm and practically lifted me off the ground. "Run," he whispered.

I ran faster than I ever had, fueled by adrenaline and sheer terror. We burst across the yard, and we were not as silent as Pablo had been. My feet kicked up leaves and rocks. My heart was beating so loudly I was sure it could be heard all the way across the Baltic Sea.

Something whistled past my ear. Ahead of me, an object clattered to the sidewalk. Gintaras and I looked down at the same moment. A knife. I turned. Pablo was behind us, running, getting closer. Startled, I nearly tripped over my own feet. The half-moon was bright overhead, but it simply is not possible that I could have seen what I nonetheless know that I saw—Pablo's vicious grin.

Gintaras ran up the sidewalk and I followed close on his heels. Ahead of us loomed the bulky ships and container stacks of the Port of Klaipeda. Behind them, the sky showed the barest hint of sunrise. The sign for the ferry showed an arrow to the left, but Gintaras went right. He led us into one of the warehouses through a side door. He ducked behind a set of gigantic steel pipes in the middle of the room and pulled me down beside him. Then he reached under his shirt and pulled a pistol from his waistband.

"Stay down," Gintaras whispered.

The warehouse door creaked open just then. My ragged breathing had slowed, but it was not back to normal. How did Pablo move so quickly? And yet so quietly? How did he know exactly where we would go? It was as if he were a cat with his vision, his sly movements and his instincts for where the mice would hide.

Could Pablo see us? I barely made out his silhouette entering through the door as I peered through a tiny space between pipes. He pulled the door shut behind him, shutting out all the light.

The door was silent. The gunshot that sounded in almost the same moment was not. I heard the bullet smack into his body. I heard Pablo grunt. Then I heard the sound of his body hitting the ground.

"Come," Gintaras said. He did not wait for me, but he did not have to.

He kept us close to walls and buildings as he led us all the way to the end of the wharf. A rusty, mid-sized barge sat rocking on the waves like an aging, overweight courtesan making one last try at attracting love. At the dock, Gintaras handed a packet to a seaman in a black toboggan. The sailor stepped aside for us to pass, whistling a signal to the men on board. Another man in a black toboggan met us as we stepped aboard, and led us into the bowels of the ship. We were shoved into a soggy metal room and the door was slammed and locked behind us from the outside.

At least in the back of the church I'd been exhausted and slept through most of our wait. Now I was awake, sitting in the cold metal room with only the dim light that filtered in through two filthy portholes.

"Where is Antanas?" I asked. "What do you know about Natalie's murder?" I had a thousand other questions, and I was ready to ask them all.

Gintaras shook his head. "Later," he said, his voice so quiet I could barely hear him. "For now, stay quiet and listen."

I tried to listen, but I wasn't sure what I should listen for. I heard the sounds of the crew moving up and down the boat. I heard gulls crying out above the ship. As the hours wore on I heard machinery come on, shut off, start up again.

I did not know how long we had been there when the sound of the engine changed and the boat began to vibrate under our feet. We were finally beginning to make our way from shore. The ship moved forward into bigger and bigger waves. As the water grew choppier, my stomach began to churn. This was my first time on the open sea, and I discovered myself to be extremely susceptible to motion sickness.

The room closed in on me and the air suddenly seemed stale. I huddled, knees up, head on knees, in a corner. Well away from shore, Gintaras finally decided to bless me with the gift of his presence. "Don't feel so good, do you?"

I refused to respond. The nausea was worse than any hangover I'd ever experienced, and I was a veteran of the worst.

Gintaras didn't speak again. I did not know if it was minutes or hours before the door finally opened. I couldn't bear to lift my head to see who had come in. Send in the KGB to cart me off to Siberia, I didn't care. At least it would be on *terra firma*.

"Bread?" Gintaras asked.

"No," I croaked, trying not to move myself in any way. He walked away. I did not look up.

How Gintaras spent his time in the hold, I do not know. I spent every minute shivering and trying not to vomit. Eventually the room went dark. It was well into the night when the door opened again.

Gintaras stood over me. "Get up, Martynas. Some fresh air will help."

I murmured and squeezed my eyes shut against the idea of moving from my dank corner.

Then there were hands under my arms, pulling at me. "Be a man, Martynas." I could hear the irritation in Gintaras's voice.

I squeezed even tighter into a ball.

Gintaras grabbed me by my armpits and bodily pulled me to my feet. "Martynas, there are some things you need to know," he said, pushing me up against the wall by my shoulders.

I started to retch.

"Pull yourself together. You'll feel better on deck, and we will talk there."

When he let go of me, I forced myself to stay upright, and I followed Gintaras through the door. We went up two flights of slippery metal stairs, coming out on the open deck. The air was cold and wet. Salt spray or rain, or both? I couldn't tell, but it felt good on my hot face. Gintaras led me to the front of the boat. The spray was heavier here, but looking out into the darkness where we were headed calmed my stomach a little.

"So this is the Baltic Sea," I said.

"Yes."

"I've never done anything like this."

Gintaras nodded. He turned his back to the spray, lit two cigarettes and handed one to me. He kept his back against the railing. I couldn't turn away from the refreshing spray, and my cigarette was soggy in moments. I threw it into the sea.

"You need to know," Gintaras said, "Antanas didn't arrange this for you."

I didn't say anything. I doubted he expected an answer.

"He thinks you're too much of a risk. He doesn't know I'm here."

If my stomach weren't churning, if I hadn't watched the murderer of my wife and her lover die on a warehouse floor the night before, if I hadn't spent three days sleeping on Užupis streets, I might have had a response. I might have had a coherent thought. I understood everything now, and anything I might have said in that moment would have been petty compared to the enormity of what was happening around me. Of what Gintaras was doing for me.

"Does he want me dead?"

Gintaras took a long drag on his cigarette. "Perhaps," he finally said. "We were forced to shut down a lot of communications lines, but I think we would have had to anyway, after everything that's happened since August 23rd. It's your valise that's the real problem. We have to assume the KGB have it and everything in it. There is also the problem of your dead American."

"What's going to happen to me?"

"That's what we need to talk about." Gintaras turned back to face the salt sea spray and rain. He tossed his spluttering cigarette into the mist. "Ordinarily, there would be people waiting for us on the other side. There is a system, and we would deliver you into it."

"Ordinarily," I echoed.

"You're not political. You did us one good deed, but you created a lot of problems for us."

"I created problems for you?" I felt my anger rise.

Gintaras shook his head. "Don't." His voice carried a warning, but the tone was sad.

I turned my back to the sea. "Do you have another cigarette?"

He lit two more cigarettes, and we smoked in silence for a time.

"Natalie was a beautiful woman," Gintaras finally said.

I took a deep breath.

"She was wise and intelligent, and she cared deeply about Lithuania."

I closed my eyes. I didn't want Gintaras to unburden himself before me, but he held my life in his hands.

"I knew her as a professor and an activist. Never as anything more."

Poor Gintaras. He was young enough to believe I cared. Was he naïve enough not to know about Indre or any of Natalie's other indiscretions? Perhaps I should call them discretions. There are the laws that govern marriage, but in truth, each marriage functions as its own unique subculture, with unwritten customs. We had been a nation of sometimes two, sometimes three, sometimes even more.

It has been said that the reason the Soviet Union survived as long as it did is because no one fully abided by its rules. If we had, the rules would have piled up one upon each other until the system collapsed.

The same is true of marriage. Only idealistic young Gintaras hadn't yet learned that.

He reached into an inside pocket in his jacket and took out a small packet of papers. He turned them over in his hands, then gave them to me. "I made a promise to Natalie. That's why you're here. There is a little cash, Swedish kroner and American dollars. Not much, but it will get you started. And a few names and addresses. The rest will be up to you."

"I'll just go to the authorities. I'm a Soviet defector," I said.

Gintaras shook his head. "You are no one. The Swedes don't want to pay for upkeep of another useless Baltic artist, and you have no political value to the Americans. And don't forget Kurt. The Americans are looking for someone to punish for his death."

As I took the packet from him, I realized just how alone I was in the world. One way or another, everyone and everything I knew had been taken from me, including Vilnius, the only lover I'd ever been faithful to.

"Look," Gintaras said, pointing out to the horizon.

I could barely see it in the edge of sunrise. Then it was there, in the distance, a hazy strip of land. "Gotland?" I asked.

"Freedom," he answered. He took a long drag on his cigarette and threw it into the sea. "Come, let's go back below deck before anyone sees us."

I followed Gintaras back to our holding cell. As we drew closer to shore and the waves subsided, my seasickness waned. Overhead and beside us, I could hear the metallic sounds of men's footsteps and shouts echoing against the hull of the ship.

I could tell from the movement of the ship that we had docked, but we were forced to wait, Gintaras pacing and me sitting quietly in my corner. I suddenly felt ravenously hungry.

After what seemed like about an hour, the door was opened from the outside. The man in the doorway was young and fit. "I'll get you around the border guards and customs," he said in Russian with a light Polish accent that reminded me of Natalie. I had barely left Lithuania, and already I was being pummeled by nostalgia. "After that, you're on your own."

Gintaras didn't answer, so I didn't either. We followed the sailor out the door, up to the deck and down to the pier.

The sky was brighter now, but it wasn't yet fully light. I could clearly see cranes and trucks moving up and down the port. We stepped onto asphalt and followed the sailor. Soon we were jogging along the shoreline. When we reached two parallel rows of cars, the Polish sailor slipped in between them and stopped. Shiny, black, brand new Mercedes Benzes. It made me dizzy to see so much unabashed wealth strewn out in the open. Gintaras and I followed him into the space between the cars. I was panting, not so much from the physical exertion as my own raw fear.

The sailor pointed to a building in the distance. Next to it was a gate in the fence. He gestured that we would go through the gate. To do that, we had to get across one last wide expanse of pavement. With his fingers, the sailor counted down: three, two, one. He took off in a burst of energy. Gintaras pointed for me to run, and then he followed.

"Martynas Kudirka!" Someone on the port shouted my name. Startled, I stumbled and fell to the ground.

"Gintaras Degutis!" the voice shouted again.

I looked up to see that Gintaras hadn't stopped for me when I fell. The sound of the voice had come from somewhere behind us. The sailor kept moving too.

A shot rang out, and then another. Ahead of me, Gintaras fell to the ground. I crawled back toward the row of cars, tearing open the skin of my hands as I scrambled to get away. I curled up behind a tire, making myself as small as I could. When I'd caught my breath, I peeked out around the edge of the Benz to look down the waterfront. There, on the shore at Port Visby, in the free and democratic country of Sweden, I watched two men pick up the body of Gintaras Degutis and toss it into the Baltic Sea. When the men straightened and looked around, I recognized them. Antanas and Stasys. I pulled back behind my tire quickly. Antanas was looking up and down the port, pistol raised in his hand. He was looking for me.

This is what Gintaras had meant.

My heart was in my throat, nearly choking me. For once in my profligate artist's life, I had done the right thing. I had chosen the far more difficult path. I had found the papers and delivered them, and had watched Indre die on a Vilnius sidewalk beside me. I had listened to the sounds of thousands of Lithuanians singing as I lay on the roof of a shed, and I had starved in the streets as I'd waited for help to arrive. This was my reward—to be hunted down like a wild animal by Antanas and Stasys, people on the same side of the struggle. These good Lithuanian people had been infected by the Soviet disease. I was not their enemy, but they would treat me as such, and the betrayal took my breath away.

More men had arrived, but they shouted in Swedish. The sound of footsteps running across the port doubled, then tripled. Antanas hesitated, then he began to run toward the gate Gintaras and I had sought. The Polish sailor must have made his escape already—I didn't see him anywhere. I did see Antanas and Stasys slip through the gate and away to freedom. Then I reached up and opened the door of the Benz nearest me and crawled in. I closed the door behind me with an expensive, quiet click and huddled on the floor in the back. Such extravagance, a car that would hold a full grown man in its wasted spaces.

I never again set foot on Lithuanian soil.

Eventually, I made my way to Stockholm and found the people whose names Gintaras had given me. Thanks to their largesse, I survived to live another day. But I owe no greater debt than to Gintaras Degutis, the man who took the bullet intended for me.

If I had known when I sat down beside him in that beige Volga two nights earlier that I would never see Vilnius again, I would have paused if only for a moment to say farewell. If I had known when I stepped onto that leaky barge at the Port of Klaipeda in the middle of the night that I was leaving Lithuania forever, well.... Perhaps I am lying to myself. The country I was leaving was a shell of its former self. There was no iron left in the wolf.

The Vilnius I loved was one I had nurtured in my imagination, despite what the Soviets and their Lithuanian lackeys had done to it. That Vilnius has never died, though it has faded as I have grown older. Perhaps I've mythologized that Vilnius, given it proportions and perspectives the real, tangible city I lived in could never contain.

I told you at the beginning of this story that in my art I was derivative and had nothing to add to what great men and women had done down through history. But on the day that I delivered Natalie's papers, I gave something back to the world, and my life changed forever because of it.

Living here as I do now in this city of clipped-wing angels, it is hard to remember a time when I had to stand in line for bread or lie on my belly atop a shaky shed roof, clutching a cheap leatherette valise to my chest, praying to a god I didn't believe in that I might live to see my country freed from the Soviets.

Most Americans can't find Lithuania on a map. You've never heard of our Singing Revolution, nor of the human chain we assembled, stretching nearly four hundred miles from my city of Vilnius, to Riga in Latvia, to Tallin in Estonia. We fought and we died for our freedom, while you wasted the freedom that is your birthright on misogynist rap lyrics, flag burning and medical marijuana.

Don't get me wrong; I love America. All of us who were forced to flee the chaos of Lithuania's tumultuous rebirth know what we gained in our new countries. But we also know what we lost. Our homes. Our culture. Friends and loved ones. Cold beet soup with warm rye bread.

I decided to put down my story in writing because I do not want to forget those things. I am an old man now, and my memories are fading. I want to remember one last time the people I have loved and lost.

For Natalie, Indre and Gintaras, I pray their souls were able to find peace.

For the old woman Vanda who shared our landing, for Žemyna my little baker girl, for all the artists I left back in Vilnius, I hope the revolution we ignited that day was good to all of them.

For Antanas, I hope you have lived the rest of your life in a godforsaken hellhole worse than the one I am now resigned to. You don't deserve the beauty and wonder of the Vilnius of my memory.

And you, my reader, I hope you can understand a little of my life and my country. In closing, I ask of you no more or less than this: remember my beloved Natalie, my beautiful city of Vilnius, and the struggle we Lithuanians fought to make ourselves free.

PART 2
EXTRAS

BOOKS

A view of love and revolution from the wrong end of a telescope

Frederick Brownloe
Special to the Times

When Martynas Kudirka's memoir *Love Songs of the Revolution* made the short list for this year's National Book Critics Circle Award for autobiography, the literary world had to scramble for the few copies still available. Its initial run had been limited, its time in bookstore windows brief. It had been, in short, an unsuccessful book. When the prize winners were announced yesterday, the chorus of adulation for Kudirka was almost as uniform as it was enthusiastic.

Almost.

Love Songs of the Revolution is a small book by a small man from a small country. The events he describes are momentous ones. Unfortunately, we would never know it by reading his book.

In the U.S., we remember the end of the Soviet Union primarily from images of the fall of the Berlin Wall. But that was only one battle in a long struggle, and many metaphorical bricks had to fall before the one of stone could. One of those bricks fell on Aug. 23, 1989, the day thousands of people across the three Baltic Soviet Republics formed a human chain nearly four hundred miles between their three capitals: from Tallinn in Estonia through Riga in Latvia to Vilnius, the capital of Lithuania.

Vilnius was home to Lithuanian Soviet realist painter and Communist Party member, Martynas Kudirka. His wife was murdered only days before the human chain demonstration, and officials were too busy trying to bottle up a revolution to search for her killer. So Kudirka took up the investigation on his own. He quickly found himself drawn into a web of political intrigue. The heartbreaking irony of his story is that the risks he ran to avenge his wife's death forced him into exile just as his beloved country was being reborn as an independent nation.

This is a revolution we should know better. Ever since then-President Mikhail Gorbachev had announced his policies of *glasnost* and *perestroika* in the early 1980s, the Soviet Union had been coming apart at its seams. The "Singing Revolution," as it is known, that swept across the Baltics in 1989, is seen by many as the tipping point that led to the Evil Empire's complete unraveling. Kudirka lived through it and may have played a significant role, but his memoir brings us neither greater understanding nor artistic pleasure.

In memoir, one common conceit is for an unknown, rather ordinary person who by happenstance bore witness to great historical events to tell the story from his or her point of view. The author personalizes the grand and systemic, bringing what was writ large on the world stage to a scale that we can understand and sympathize with. Kudirka has taken this to an extreme. Instead of making the breakup of the Soviet Union comprehensible, he has trivialized a revolution until we cannot care about it.

As a narrator, Kudirka is narcissistic and arrogant. In the moments when he seems poised to share some important detail about Lithuania and its revolution, he chooses to tell some trivial detail about himself. As a protagonist, he is unreliable and unhelpful. The dissonance between some of his more lofty thoughts and his almost uniformly petty actions grows ever louder as the story develops:

Perhaps espionage comes naturally to some men. I would have expected it to come easily to me. Sneaking around with other women so that Natalie didn't learn of my affairs had been so simple. A white lie here, an evasion there. Slipping out of clothes late at night in the kitchen.

Treading carefully to avoid certain squeaky floorboards. Turning corners at just the right moment to make sure I wasn't seen by this friend or that.

Making sure one wasn't followed when taking incriminating documents to i n d e p e n d e n c e activists was another task entirely. I had no training in this.

To be fair, as an accidental spy, Kudirka's work can't compare to that of professional agents who turned their lives to memoir, like Floyd Paseman, Antonio J. Mendez and the husband-wife team of Robert and Dayna Baer. What's more, he writes in the uncomfortably long shadow of fiction writers who have brought espionage so dramatically to life that true spy stories sometimes pale by comparison.

In fact, there are large parts of Kudirka's memoir that read more like John Le Carré or Alan Furst than truth. This seems particularly relevant in light of the CIA's statement issued earlier this week that none of their agents were killed in Lithuania in 1989. It raises awkward questions about what Kudirka fictionalized, and to what degree. The ghost of James Frey's *A Million Little Pieces* hovers over this book. Even if major publishers are comfortable blurring the line between memoir and fiction in pursuit of sales and the bottom line, major literary awards committees have a responsibility to ensure their nonfiction prizes are awarded to writers who rely on fact and skilled telling of truths, not writers of fiction.

Whether his book is fact or highly fictionalized memories, Kudirka's one saving grace is his brutal honesty as he admits to all his weaknesses and infidelities, personal, political and artistic. If your experience of Soviet-era storytelling led you to believe that all artists were dissidents who fought the power of the state at every turn, Kudirka offers a refreshing antidote. Some artists happily accepted everything the state had to offer, giving up artistic freedom for creature comforts and popular adulation:

> *Most of the great and good artists I knew— Eastern or Western, Baltic or Russian— opposed their governments to one degree or another. I, on the other hand, was a second rate talent. When mimicking the works of others, my hand was supple. When charged with responsibility for my own style, my wrists and knuckles froze like those of an arthritic old bachelor. I expect this memoir will show me to be much the same in the literary arts.*

In the light of Cold War nostalgia running rampant on both sides of the former Iron Curtain, selection of this book for the National Book Critics Circle Award seems almost jingoistic. Kudirka's story would have played well to American audiences in the Reagan era. How this memoir is received in Lithuania and other parts of the former Soviet Union may tell us something about the state of relations between the two great former superpowers nearly 30 years on.

Frederick Brownloe is, most recently, author of **Fade to White: A History of Espionage in the Antarctic.**

CantorCan Blog

Photo by Delaney Cantor

October 9

What with "Love Songs of the Revolution" getting so much attention these days - and it's set in Lithuania the year I was born! - I thought I'd pick it up and do the same analysis on it that I've been doing with Soviet-era Eastern European novels for my dissertation. Turns out the book is full of big surprises. Not good ones. I know people sometimes play fast & loose with their memoirs, but it seems egregious here. This book claims to be a memoir, but I can usually find more historical facts in those novels than I can in Love Songs.

The biggest, reddest flag in the book is the set of documents Kudirka finds in the chicken coop (a little too convenient, no?). All through my childhood, I heard so many stories from my grandmother's friends about the Singing Revolution and how they threw out the Soviets. They didn't do it with a "valise" stuffed

ABOUT ME
I believe books can change the world. Watch me prove it by following my adventures as I write my dissertation.
Read more...

QUOTE
"Poets may be delightful creatures in the meadow or the garret, but they are menaces on the assembly line."

From The Courage to Create by Rollo May

READING NOW
Headed for the Blues by Josef Skvorecky

READING NEXT
On the Road to Babadag by Andrzej Stasiuk

TAGS
Albania
Authors
Autobiography
Baltic
Books

with nonspecific "documents." So many Lithuanian men and women took incredible risks to hold illegal meetings, and to get out in the streets and protest. I even interviewed some of those people for a history paper I wrote as an undergrad. They took those same risks over and over again, getting caught, punished, and still refusing to be silenced. You can't overthrow a government by blackmailing them with a bunch of documents, no matter how damning those documents might be. It's like thinking you can overthrow a government by tweeting about how much you don't like it. It's not enough to have the words or even the facts on your side.

Even with the Soviet-era novels I've been analyzing, it wasn't the novels that created political change. Those books provided an alternative analysis and helped their readers to see the oppression for what it was. But that only helped to create a fallow ground where political dissidents and activists could organize people to take actions that would change the world. The novelists I've talked to who were writing in those days saw themselves as playing a limited role in a much broader political movement.

But it gets worse. I've just run across an article by a history prof who raises pointed questions about the people Kudirka names in the book. He says—and I agree—they're just a little too familiar:

- Martynas **Kudirka**: Vincas Kudirka was a poet who wrote the country's national anthem
- Natalie **Milosz**: Czeslaw Milosz won the 1980 Nobel Prize for literature
- Indre **Bučienė**: the real name of Salome Neris, a very famous Lithuanian woman poet from the 1900s

And Žemyna—the name of his "little baker"—is the name of the goddess of the earth in traditional Lithuanian mythology.

It's starting to look like this guy has written what's basically a self-aggrandizing work of fiction to try to take personal credit for overthrowing the Soviets. He completely diminishes the work of all those amazing people like Vytautas Landsbergis and Kazimira Prunskienė and all the unnamed people who fought their way to freedom. It's just not right.

Maybe I'm taking it a little too personally because it's Lithuania, but I want to get to the bottom of this.

Comments

Josef said...
Have you considered the characters' first names? First book ever published in the Lithuanian language was The Simple Words of Catechism, 1547 by Martynas Mazvydas. Coincidence?

Anna said...
You should totally apply for a Fulbright to go research this in Lithuania.

notkenkesey said...
If you're serious about this for your dissertation, I'd dig a little deeper into this "Lithuanian Soviet Realism" crap. Doesn't exist.

CantorCan said...
Thanks for the pointers, @Josef and @notkenkesey. I'll keep digging for more details. @Anna—I'm going to do it. I've just downloaded the Fulbright application forms. Keep your fingers crossed for me!

A real Lithuanian said...
Seriously. Love Songs reads like a bad

Le Carré knockoff. Anybody who knows Vilnius in the 1980s can punch holes in the story by page ten.

Gerald said...

Ms. "CantorCan," I recommend you review my article in the Journal of Baltic Studies before going any further. My exploration of the national archives in Vilnius finds no evidence of the life of either Martynas Kudirka or Natalie Milosz, nor evidence of any couple who match their particulars. Furthermore, there are no records of murders on the day of the human chain across the Baltics. Utilizing Bell's oral histories of Lithuanian visual artists, I identified several individuals in Lithuania and the US who could possibly be the actual "Kudirka." I have interviewed and eliminated all of them from consideration. The Kudirka question may be much larger than you think.

EXTRA NO. 3

Atmostas Baltija, Bunda Jau Baltija, Ärgake Baltimaad
(The Baltics Are Waking Up)

The Baltics Are Waking Up! (Lithuanian: ***Bunda jau Baltija,*** Latvian: ***Atmostas Baltija***, Estonian: ***Ärgake, Baltimaad***) **is a trilingual Baltic song composed for the occasion of the Baltic Way, a large demonstration against the Soviet Union and for independence of the Baltic States in commemoration of the 50th anniversary of Molotov-Ribbentrop Pact. The song is sometimes called the 'general anthem of the Baltics'. The Lithuanian text was sung by Žilvinas Bubelis, Latvian by Viktors Zemgalis, Estonian by Tarmo Pihlap. —Wikipedia**

English translation of *The Baltics Are Waking Up!*

Sung in Latvian
Three sisters stand by the coast of sea
They are pressed by weakness and tiredness.
Their lands and spirits crushed,
And the honour and sense of three nations.

But in towers the bells of destiny toll,
And the sea starts to wave.
Three sisters wake up from sleep,
Come to stand for themselves.

The Baltics are waking up, the Baltics are waking up
Lithuania, Latvia, Estonia!

Sung in Lithuanian
Three sisters sleep by the sea

They are pressed by the bond, desperation
Wandering like a beggar by the sea coast
The spirit of nations' honour

But the bell of the destiny rings again
And the sea tousles its waves
Three sisters wake from the sleep
To defend their honour.

The Baltics are waking up, the Baltics are waking up,
Lithuania, Latvia, Estonia!

Sung in Estonian
Three sisters with faces of sea,
They were made sleepy by the song of waves.
Three nations fighting here for centuries
Sacrificed ancient honour.

When the bells ring in towers,
The sea is taken by the will of freedom.
To protect the fate and life,
Three sisters wake now.

Wake up Baltic countries,
Lithuania, Latvia, Estonia!

Delaney Cantor's Twitter feed

@vilnaquest

No matter how big your suitcase is, you'll fill it. So maybe I'll just take another one!
9:26 PM Aug 14th

Barely made my connection at JFK. Grateful for free wifi at Helsinki. Hard to believe I'll be in Kudirka's "beloved Vilnius" soon
10:33 AM Aug 22nd

Good point @profjentry - he could actually be a she. I still think he's a he, but I've got to keep an open mind
10:37 AM Aug 22nd

Host family was great. Just found an awesome apt- tiny, but good location & within my budget. Serious research begins now!
8:27 AM Sept 18th

Yes @markybark I've tried Svyturys and Kalnapilis. Utenos seems pretty popular. Light, kind of pilsner-ish
9:57 PM Sept 25th

Found a building in Žirmūnai EXACTLY like Natalie's lab from Love Songs! Having coffee in a nearby cafe, newsstand out front.
10:55 AM Oct 2nd

Got brave, walked in the front door. Just a bunch of offices. Was it ever a lab? #feelingkindadown
11:48 AM Oct 2nd

First visit to the archives set for tomorrow. Fingers crossed, everybody
9:57 PM Oct 4th

Confirmed: no Martynas Kudirka, Natalie Milosz or Indre Bučienė in the archives
12:05 PM Oct 5th

Bigger news: did find a Gintaras Degutis in the archives. Son of an army general! Disappeared from Lith records 1989
12:08 PM Oct 5th

Thank your mom for the tip @jailbreak57 The šaltnosiukai were amazing. Love those "nosy" Lithuanian lingonberries
2:13 PM Oct 7th

Don't know @danalok. Degutis as author or murderer?
2:15 PM Oct 7th

Been a while, I know. Lots of interviews re: Degutis et al. So far all dead ends
11:16 AM Dec 18th

No water in my apt for 3 days! Landlord says
maybe fixed by tomorrow. WTF am I supposed to
do in the meantime?
8:05 PM Dec 20th

No @profjentry. Maybe half the people I've
interviewed know about Love Songs. Seems most
Lithuanians think it was made up by an American
11:27 AM Dec 21st

Thanks for asking @danalok water finally back on
this a.m. & had the best bath ever
11:29 AM Dec 21st

Had a big interview with 1980s independence
activist today—said he knew Degutis. Never heard
of Love Songs or Martynas Kudirka
3:52 PM Dec 29th

He described this scene: 3 men escaping down
back alleys from Baltic Way demo, climbing up wall
& onto shed to hide!!!!!
3:56 PM Dec 29th

Knew 3 different guys named "Antanas" in the
movement
4:07 PM Dec 29th

Says Degutis disappeared right after human chain—none of the fmr indep activists have ever seen him since. Suspicious!
4:15 PM Dec 29th

OK @profjentry You're prob'ly right. Going "radio silent"
4:21 PM Dec 29th

Naujųjų Metų! (Happy New Year!)
12:19 AM Jan 1st

Back to archives yesterday on a hunch. Mixed & matched names, found an "Antanas Kudirka"
11:29 AM Jan 5th

This AK was a low-level KGB functionary in 1989. Can't be coincidence, can it?
11:32 AM Jan 5th

AK emigrated to US in 1994. Hope we got lots of good info from him for taking in ex-KGB
11:36 AM Jan 5th

Sorry @danalok it's all interviews & digging thru archives-no time to blog. Best I can do is tweet every now & again. Miss you too!
11:52 AM Jan 5th

LOVE SONGS OF THE REVOLUTION

Got a strange call from woman says she knows
who Kudirka really is. Sounded kooky, but I can't
turn down the chance #lotsahope
9:19 AM Jan 8th

Of course @profjentry I'm always careful. We meet
tomorrow 3 pm in my fave cafe
9:33 AM Jan 11th

Waiting for the interview. Hope she's for real. Mr.
Kudirka, I will find out who you are!
2:54 PM Jan 12th

If I'm lucky, maybe she knows Degutis too
3:05 PM Jan 12th

Also, water off again in the apt. How long will they
take to fix it this time?
3:22 PM Jan 12th

No, @danalok, still waiting.
3:49 PM Jan 12th

Guess it's going to be back to the archives. I
should do a deeper dive on Degutis anyway.
4:18 PM Jan 12th

Damn wasted afternoon. Been in this cafe 2 hrs
now. Looks like she's not going to show & I don't
have her phone number. I'm #outtahere
5:08 PM Jan 12th

Film News
Posted: Jan 6, 3:52pm PT

Doug Liman to produce and direct 'Love Songs of the Revolution'

'Bourne' director to helm controversial Cold War thriller

By TINA SEAGAL

Doug Liman is taking on controversial Cold War thriller "Love Songs of the Revolution," the award-winning book that introduced Americans to Lithuania.

Liman will also be producing through the Hypnotic banner, along with longtime collaborator Avram Ludwig. Tony Gilroy, lead author on the Bourne trilogy, wrote the adaptation.

The story centers on a Soviet artist whose wife is murdered and finds himself drawn into Cold War espionage. The year is 1989, and the artist searches for his wife's killers amidst growing pro-independence protests that rocked the country that year and ultimately led to the collapse of the Soviet Union.

Warner Bros. originally considered the project, but nagging questions about the identity of the author and veracity of the book—it was marketed as memoir and won the National Book Critics Circle award for autobiography— eventually led them to back out. The book's publisher, Random House, recently issued a statement reporting that "Martynas Kudirka" is in fact a pseudonym. The publishing powerhouse continues to stand by the book as a memoir.

As one Warner executive told us, "No question, Love Songs is a great story, and it will make a fantastic movie, but it has that unpleasant 'Misha-raised-by-wolves' taint that has scared off a lot of good directors."

Though not Liman, who's no stranger to controversy. He returned from what he called a "fact-finding mission" to Lithuania last month. He says his discovery of police records about the unsolved 1989 murder of an American named Kurt Parable in a small Lithuanian town was the ultimate deciding point for him.

"For every fact that isn't true in the book, we find a truth hiding underneath it," he said. "It's a great story. In Martynas Kudirka we have an anti-hero people can identify with who becomes a true hero."

No word yet on who will play the Kudirka role.

Random House is closely guarding the name of the book's author, despite heated speculation and debate within the literary community.

Liman's previous credits include "Attica," "Fair Game," "The Bourne Identity," "Mr. and Mrs. Smith" and "Jumper."

CAA represents Liman.

Contact the Variety newsroom at news@variety.com

EXTRA NO. 6

Excerpt from the memoir of Col. Alastair Robbins, Air Force (ret.),
My Cold War, published by the author in 1995

In March of 1989 I had a young visitor to my home, asking questions about that fateful year, 1960. Perhaps I should have expected him or someone of his ilk, based on all the mysteries I witnessed that year.

The young man's name was Kurt Parable, and when he first telephoned me, he did not have to say his name twice before I knew exactly the "why" of his call. Despite my misgivings—I knew things he would not want to hear—I agreed to meet the young man in three days' time at a local park. No matter what he wanted, this was my opportunity. Finally, someone would listen to me and what I knew. But we had to meet in the open, away from the listening devices and prying eyes.

"Colonel Robbins," the young man said, and I quote exactly, because by then I had learned to take detailed notes of every conversation I had related to the events of 1960. The spiral notebooks that contain these notes are stored and catalogued in a safe place offsite from the homestead. I have retrieved the relevant notebooks for the purpose of writing this memoir, and will return them to their place of safety as soon as this task is complete.

"Colonel Robbins," the young man said to me in the park that day, "my name is Kurt Parable, and I believe you knew my father, Robert Parable."

I had in fact known his father, so I answered in the affirmative. In 1960 Robert had been a leading aerospace engineer for the Lockheed Corporation, assigned to the then-secret U-2 project.

The young man continued. "When we buried what was left of my father in 1960, we were told that he had died in a crash near Edwards Air Force Base in California."

"Yes," I answered. I kept my answer short. Kurt was correct in that this was the story we had been told to tell.

"They told my mother that he died when a test version of a new NASA weather airplane he was working on crashed in the desert."

"Yes," I reiterated.

"Supposedly, my father was on that plane."

"Your father loved to fly, and he was notorious for sneaking onto test flights of the planes he designed." Anyone who knew Robert Parable knew this about him.

"Now, Colonel, I know you have your orders. Or at least you did. But you are retired and thirty years have passed. I deserve the truth now." The hope in his eyes went straight to my heart.

I knew what young Kurt was getting at. By 1961, everyone knew the "NASA weather airplane" story had been a cover, and a weak one at that. When the Soviets displayed before the international press the U-2 they had shot down, its component parts from stem to stern stamped with Air Force insignia, the game was up. The US had been sending spy planes criss-crossing enemy skies for years. When the Soviets paraded the U-2 pilot, Captain Francis Gary Powers, through their kangaroo courts, that was just the icing on the cake that would destroy his career. His story is by now well known.

What had happened to Lockheed engineer Robert Parable, however, has never been told.

I was on the tarmac at the Badaber US Air Station in Peshawar in the early morning hours on May 1, 1960, and watched Powers take off on his ill-fated Operation Grand Slam flight.

I had also been on the tarmac two weeks earlier when another U-2 had taken off in Operation Cloud Burst. The history books say this flight was cancelled due to bad weather, and for other reasons that have not yet been declassified.

This is not true. What is classified is not information about a U-2 flight that did not take off, but about a flight that did. One that did not reach its destination.

Operation Cloud Burst had been a final test flight for a new design of the U-2, a two-seater that would allow for more direct manipulation of the photography equipment by a second person. Parable had been the lead designer of that plane, so he was in Peshawar for the test run.

The talk amongst CIA cognoscenti was that President Eisenhower might cut back on U-2 spy flights in advance of the Four Powers Summit, for fear of provoking an armed incident between the United States and the Soviets, so they wanted to get as many planes in the air taking as many photos as possible before the ax fell. That's why the two-seater U-2 was on the tarmac at Peshawar the morning of April 19, prepped for a formal mission.

What exactly happened to Parable, not even I know that. What I do know—and I decided his son Kurt had the right to know—is that the experimental U-2 went down over Lithuania. When a secret CIA rescue mission went looking for the pilot, he was nowhere to be found.

I will lay out the facts as they are known to me, and as I laid them out for Kurt Parable that day in the park:

- The experimental U-2 used for Operation Cloud Burst crashed in Lithuania.
- The Soviets never announced the crash, or the discovery of the plane and its occupants.
- The CIA, which ran the U-2 program, has never acknowledged the crash or even the existence of Operation Cloud Burst.
- Neither the pilot of the U-2 nor Robert Parable was ever

seen after that flight.

- Soon after Operation Cloud Burst, a standard U-2 flown by Captain Francis Gary Powers on Operation Grand Slam was brought down by Soviet pilots over Russian territory.
- A false cover story about Parable's death was issued quietly by Lockheed three days after Powers's plane went down.
- The month after the Powers debacle, I received a rather unexpected promotion and was transferred to Edwards Air Force Base.
- Within six months, Soviet high-altitude reconnaissance planes had gone through a major redesign and were reaching altitudes American intelligence experts had estimated would take them at least seven years to achieve.
- The experimental two-seat version of the U-2 was scrapped immediately.
- At the time of the Operation Cloud Burst crash, Lockheed had been in the midst of negotiating a separate sole-source contract with the Air Force for a new fighter jet. Those negotiations were shut down immediately, but two months later the Air Force opened negotiations for an almost identical jet fighter program with Boeing.

I told these facts to Kurt Parable. When I was done, the young man looked me full-on and asked, "Was my father on that plane?"

It was 1989, and nearly thirty Cold War years had passed since his father's airplane had crashed. In that time, no one—not the Soviets, the CIA or Lockheed—had ever acknowledged that question, much less answered it. For that reason, I told Kurt the truth I believed he deserved.

"Did I see your father get on that airplane? No. Was he on it? He must have been."

"Is it possible that he survived the crash?"

To me the facts add up to a clear and obvious answer to that question. But people like me who piece together the facts of a situation and speak the obvious aloud are called "conspiracy theorists." For years, I went through proper channels in the Air Force to share my concerns. I respected the chain of command as was my responsibility. I understood that to serve the greater good of protecting Our Great Nation, some secrets must be kept.

To my shock and dismay, no one would listen to me. Did they prefer to close their eyes to the threat this plane crash had created to our peace and freedom? One of America's greatest aerospace engineers was now working for the Soviets! It was manifestly evident—the Soviets had captured Parable and somehow turned him.

No! The American government preferred to deal with the blowback rather than admit to the mistake that had created it.

When the Soviet Union collapsed in 1991 we did not experience an opening of the books or a clearing of the decks. Oh, we pretended to, on both sides of the Iron Curtain. But they did not free Parable, and we did not admit to Operation Cloud Burst. Men like Parable who should have been held to account for their treasonous acts were left under the rugs they'd been swept beneath. Instead of shining a light on the evils of the Cold War era so that wrongs could be righted, secrets were kept secret and misguided naiveté reigned even as it had before.

I had spent my career fighting the Soviets and serving my country, and this New World Order was not what I had dreamed of. I retired and settled down to write my memoir. A story, it turns out, that no major publishing house was brave enough to take on. When I published my book, even the bookstores were too yellow to carry it.

The truth is the truth, and as a man of faith who loves his country, I have an obligation to the truth as I know it. I have written it on these pages, as I told it to Kurt that day.

"Your father survived the crash, and when he did, he went to work for the Soviets."

As I expected, Kurt grew angry with me. How could I possibly believe a man like his father would go to work for the enemy?

"Your father was a brilliant engineer, and he understood politics as well as he did airplanes. That is why he was so successful at Lockheed. When his plane crashed and no one from the United States came looking for him—which was a crime, no doubt about that—he made a decision to survive. That was his mistake. He should have taken his own life rather than work for the Soviets."

Kurt may not have liked what he learned about his father that day, but he thanked me for my honesty.

I heard from the young man one last time, later in the year. He called to let me know he had secured a visa and booked a flight to Vilnius. He had decided to go search for his father. And thus in the summer of 1989, Kurt Parable disappeared into the belly of the Soviet beast. Like his father, he was never seen again.

From Gawker.com

MOVIES
Could This Man Write a Love Song?

Dick Lawless — An elderly Lithuanian-American man named Antanas Kudirka (above) has been discovered living a quiet life in the LA neighborhood of Atwater Village. Some say he's the author of the award-winning *Love Songs of the Revolution*. Others say he's a murderer. This elderly Kudirka seems befuddled and confused by the media circus in his front yard. He appeared on his porch this morning, two bulky men with conspicuous lumps under their jackets by his side. He made one quick statement to the press in a heavy Eastern European accent, before going back inside: "If you want to find a murderer, talk to Gintaras Degutis."

Which might be rather difficult, since Degutis disappeared 1989. He is presumed dead.

Read more

EXTRA NO. 8
Deleted scenes

Deleted from Chapter 1

It was no use. She was dead. Staring into her half-mast eyes, almost willing them to open, I reached to take her right hand. Instead of skin, though, I felt paper.

Clenched in the fist where I'd sought comfort was a rolled-up sheaf of papers. I took the papers and flattened them between my own two hands. A student paper with a failing grade written on the top, beside the title: "Two-dimensional system response to unit-step input." My wife may have been beautiful and brilliant, but radiophysics was truly dull.

I glanced through the first few lines of the paper and even I with my limited understanding of science could see that the grade was well earned. Then I saw the name across the top of the page: Gintaras Degutis. My heart thudded to a stop.

Of all the student names that could be on a paper in my dead wife's hand, why did it have to be his? I was instantly transported back a few weeks to a Saturday morning when Natalie had announced she would have to go into the office. The look in her eyes when she had said that could not have been clearer. Wherever she was going, it did not involve radiophysics.

"To the office?" I'd answered, before I could stop myself. I looked back down into my coffee cup so that she would not see the look in my eyes. We had made accommodations in our marriage, she for me and I for her. It must have been indigestion from a heavy dinner the night before. Ordinarily, I would never have said those words aloud, even if they had crossed my mind.

Natalie turned off the water and put down the dish she had been washing. "To the office," she said softly. A quiet echo that sounded nothing like my proud wife. I looked up and met her eyes.

The sweet, burning glow of jealousy in my solar plexus burst into flames. The breath behind her whisper had been like the blow of bellows on a smoldering log. "With whom will you be working in the lab on a beautiful Saturday afternoon?" I used precision grammar like a sharp, powerful weapon.

"A student. A bright one with a future."

As if to say I had none.

"His name?" Before she could answer, I realized my mistake. "Or should I ask for her name?" Natalie's view of Soviet gender equality extended from the workplace into the bedroom, which was unusual for a Party member.

This was not the first time we had had an exchange like this, but I had never seen Natalie react in quite the way she was now. There were tears in her eyes. They frightened me. If she had shot back with pithy witticisms, or attacked me back for my own indiscretions, I would have known how to respond. Natalie did not cry often, and certainly not over something so mundane as a simple affair of the body. The partnership my wife and I had built over the years was on a solid bedrock of mutual respect, leavened with enough love to give it a little pizazz.

I was looking into the eyes of a woman who had fallen in love with someone else.

"For god's sake, just give me a name," I said.

"Gintaras," she said. To her credit, she held herself together and did not let the tears fall.

"Tell me where you met this Gintaras," I said. I did my wife the courtesy of growing neither angry nor maudlin. I wanted facts.

"He really is a student of mine. Not one of the brighter ones."

"Oh."

Now that I knew this fact, I wondered what I should do with it. Of course students would fall in love with my wife. She was beautiful, intelligent, accomplished, a Party member. But the less-than-stellar student my wife had fallen for, was he worthy of her in any way?

"Gintaras who? Do I know him?"

She did not answer immediately. I waited while Natalie took a deep breath, looked down at her fingernails, flicked a bit of invisible fluff from her pink blouse, then looked up at me.

"Degutis," she said.

My heart skipped a beat. That was a name I could never imagine being spoken in our home. "You can't mean the son of General Degutis."

She took hold of the edge of the sink behind her and looked up at the wall, but said nothing.

"Your uncles," I said. Still she did not speak. "The Forest Brothers," I said, raising my voice.

Natalie looked at me, eyebrows raised. I was veering into dangerous territory. The Forest Brothers were a band of Lithuanian fighters who'd carried on a guerrilla war against the Soviets in the Joniškis forests well into the mid-1960s. I'd been raised—and Natalie had too—to know that you couldn't talk about what you couldn't talk about. This was one of those things. Even those who'd supported the Forest Brothers' struggle didn't like to claim them. Both sides in their war of attrition had been guilty of shocking brutality, and many lives had been lost. Including two of Natalie's uncles. They may have been Brothers, they may not. Natalie had never told me, and I had been enough of a good Soviet not to ask.

"What did the KGB call what General Degutis' troops were doing, 'clean-up operations?'" I said. But it wasn't a question. "Like they were a bit of dust, some spilled milk." It was a bald-faced taunt.

"Don't visit the sins of the father upon the son," Natalie said, her cheeks flushing in anger.

"The apple never falls far from the tree," I answered in retort.

"In that, you are very wrong," Natalie said. Her fists tightened on the edge of the sink. "Remember last year, when that small band of protesters raised the Lithuanian flag over Gediminas Tower?"

How could I forget? No one could. It had been the first time in thirty years that the Lithuanian flag had been flown over the city of Vilnius.

Natalie pushed herself away from the sink now, leaning forward a little as she did when pressing her position in an argument. "The general was ordered to send in his troops. Gintaras talked his father into standing down."

So he was brave as well. I swallowed hard. "And your feelings for him...." I broke off before I could say those terrible words.

Natalie cocked her head a little, as if surprised or confused by my words. "Haven't you been listening?" she asked. "I love him."

Deleted from Chapter 7

The crowds in and around Cathedral Square were larger than I'd imagined. How was it possible so many people knew about the human chain? How many more knew about it but were sitting at home too afraid to venture out?

Then again, how many in the crowd were police, informants, intelligence, spies?

Families in the crowd were dressed in a mix of formality, women in skirts and blouses, men in suit jackets and matching trousers. They dressed their younger children much the same. Teenagers, though, wore the latest western fashions: blue jeans and black vinyl jackets, sleeves pulled up to their elbows, collars turned up. The teenage girls and some of the boys wore their hair teased up and around their heads, held in place with clips and rubber bands. Old ladies wrapped their heads in kerchiefs. Here and there stood groups of women and men dressed in traditional Lithuanian clothes with puffed peasant sleeves and round white hats with folk stitching around the sides. From time to time these groups would break into traditional Lithuanian folk songs. When they did, the crowds around them joined in.

A sudden movement to my right caught my eye. A man in a mismatched set of blue trousers and a lighter blue jacket stepped up onto the low retaining wall behind us. He wore cheap, black plastic sandals and red socks on his feet. He put a cassette into his square boom box and snapped it shut with a flourish, shouting, "*Bunda jau Baltija!*"

"*Laisvė!*" several people in the crowd called out, with a few shouting along in English, "Freedom!" Then the opening chords of the new but familiar song began.

"Turn it up!" someone shouted.

The man in the blue suit turned the volume knob and lifted the boom box high overhead.

"Three sisters stand by the coast of the sea," the song began. A few people muttered along with the Latvian lyrics.

Trīs māsas jūras malā stāv,
Tās nespēks un nogurums māc.

I groaned inwardly. How could anyone think that a song could change the world? Even a hundred songs about freedom and democracy couldn't overcome the bare-knuckle power wielded by our Soviet overlords. Words aren't power. Art isn't power. If it were I would know. Power is power. A song in three languages about three sisters waking up from a deep sleep couldn't compete with brute Soviet force. It was nothing more than cheap rock anthem triumphalism.

Most of the conversations around the man in the blue suit had fallen silent. When *Baltija* came to the Lithuanian lyrics, everyone around me took up the tune and sang along. Men and women in their tight-fitting blue jeans shouted the words at the tops of their lungs, holding each other's hands overhead.

> *Three sisters wake from the sleep*
> *To defend their honour.*
> *The Baltics are waking up, the Baltics are waking up,*
> *Lithuania, Latvia, Estonia!*

Not surprisingly, the chorus faded to a mutter with the Estonian lyrics.

When the last chords of the song faded, a cheer went up all around me. It spread throughout Cathedral Square. I took the opportunity to slip away to the place I'd come to find.

They could sing all they wanted. I had the papers that would make the revolution come true.

Deleted from Chapter 9

The sky was brighter now, but it wasn't yet fully light. I could clearly see cranes and trucks moving up and down the port. We stepped onto asphalt and followed the sailor to the right. Soon we were almost running along the shoreline. When we reached two parallel rows of cars, the Polish sailor slipped in between them and stopped. Shiny, black, brand new Mercedes Benzes. It made me dizzy to see so much unabashed wealth strewn out in the open. Gintaras and I followed him into the space between the cars. I was panting, not so much from the physical exertion as my own raw fear.

The sailor pointed to a building in the distance. Next to it was a gate in the fence. He gestured that we would go through the gate. To do that, we had to get across one last wide expanse of pavement. With his fingers, the sailor counted down: three, two, one. He took off in a burst of energy. Gintaras pointed for me to run, and then he followed.

We had almost made it to the gate when someone on the port shouted my name, "Martynas Kudirka!"

"Gintaras Degutis!" the voice shouted again.

I looked up to see Gintaras fall to his knees and roll across the pavement back toward the far end of the row of cars. I thought of his father the general training young recruits to drop and roll, clutching rifles to their chests. A shot rang out. I had never had such training, but I dropped and rolled too.

When I was safely behind a Benz tire, I looked over at Gintaras. He was sitting up, back against the other tire, pistol in both hands. His face looked grim, determined, unafraid.

"I know you are there, hiding behind the cars."

As I gasped to regain my breath, I leaned out around the edge of the Benz to see what was happening. There on the waterfront of Port Visby, in the free and democratic country of Sweden, the sailor who had been leading us to safety was lying inert on the pavement, arms and legs sprawled.

A shot rang out and I pulled back behind the tire quickly. Another shot followed.

"Don't stick your head out, fool," Gintaras said.

He shifted his grip on the pistol a little. Then he leaned

down to his right, looking under the car. It only took a second before he was back behind the tire.

"Damn. I can't see anything."

The other man shouted again. "Give us Kudirka, and you can go. We don't care what you do with your miserable life."

"Bullshit," Gintaras muttered.

"How can the KGB be here in Sweden?" I asked. My throat was dry, and it came out as a whisper.

Gintaras looked over at me. "You don't recognize his voice?"

I shook my head, afraid my voice might fail me entirely.

"It's Antanas."

Earlier on the ship, I had asked if Antanas wanted me dead. Now I realized I hadn't meant it at all. When faced with the very real possibility of my death, I could not imagine it. I was a second-rate painter and a third-rate functionary of no importance whatsoever.

But even more than all that, I was struck by the improbability that a valise full of documents could weaken the Soviets' grip on power. For government officials to be blackmailed, they would have to care about how they were viewed in the world, and the sum of my lifetime's experiences told me they would not.

Yet there I sat, leaning against a whitewall tire on Gotland Island in the middle of the Baltic Sea. Another shot rang out. I felt the Benz shake as the bullet hit.

Gintaras looked around the car to his left. "It's not far to the gate," he whispered. "When I say so, get over here quickly, behind me."

We waited several minutes in silence. A flock of seagulls that had taken off in alarm with the first gunshots began to settle down one by one along the waterfront. Then, suddenly there was the sound of feet running.

"Now!" Gintaras whispered urgently as he jumped to his

feet and fired his gun twice. Antanas answered with a shot of his own. I scrambled toward Gintaras, and by the time he was squatted back down I was in front of him behind the other tire.

"They've moved that way," Gintaras pointed to his right. "Next time they move, they'll be behind us, and we'll be exposed. We have to go now."

"Go where?"

"The gate."

And without a moment to let me give my own opinion of his plan, Gintaras grabbed me by the shirt and said, "Stay close. We go now."

He practically lifted me to my feet as he rose to his, still holding me by the shirt with one hand, pistol in the other.

As we ran toward the gate, I tried to mimic the way this well-trained general's son held his body hunched over. Gunshots rang out. A bullet whizzed by my ear. Gintaras was shooting too.

As we made the gate, I heard a cry of pain and shock. I turned to see Antanas fall to the ground.

"Don't stop!" Gintaras shouted.

We made it through the gate, but Gintaras didn't stop until there was a warehouse between us and the place where Antanas lay. Within moments, two men in uniforms were standing in front of us, rifles raised, shouting at us in Swedish. Then German. Then English.

Gintaras raised his arms, then slowly leaned over to lay his gun on the ground. And smiled. We would survive.

JUSTICE FOR DELANEY

Candlelight vigil in memory of Delaney Cantor
May 22 at 7:30 pm
Bruin Plaza

Graduate student Delaney Cantor
Our friend and sister
*Murdered while conducting Fulbright research
in Lithuania*

Her death reminds us
no woman is free from violence until all women are

From Lithuania to Los Angeles
Women have the right to be safe from harm
At work, on the streets and in their homes

Please join us as we stand up for the rights of all women everywhere!
ASL INTERPRETATION AVAILABLE

Memorials for Delaney Cantor can be left on her Facebook page

EXTRA NO. 10

Press release from the Association of Free Lithuanian Patriots in America

FOR IMMEDIATE RELEASE
Memorial to Lithuanian freedom fighters to be unveiled in Cleveland

CLEVELAND, OH—A memorial to Lithuanians who died in the struggle for freedom during the Soviet era will be unveiled two weeks from today at the Lithuanian Cultural Garden in Cleveland, Ohio. This memorial, a statue of an iron wolf, was established by the Association of Free Lithuanian Patriots in America.

"The iron wolf is an important symbol in the history of Lithuania and especially our capital, Vilnius. It is a symbol of the strength of those who fought for our freedom," explained Romaldus Simonavičius, president of the AFLPA. "By making it part of this garden in Cleveland, we make it part of the American story as well."

According to Lithuanian legend, in the early 1300s, the Lithuanian Grand Duke Gediminas went hunting in a sacred forest. While asleep in the forest that night, he dreamt of an iron wolf on a hill, surrounded by hundreds more wolves. The Grand Duke's advisors interpreted his dream to refer to a castle and city that would become the capital of the Lithuanian nation. He eventually did build the city of Vilnius on the site where he had seen the Iron Wolf in his dreams. Today, Vilnius is the capital of Lithuania.

As part of the unveiling ceremony, the names of Lithuanians who died in the struggle will be read aloud.

"As the years pass, memories fade. We forget the struggle against the Soviets and what these men and women did for their country," said Simonavičius. "Then one day we awake to find freedom fighters like Gintaras Degutis being insulted, accused of murder or worse. But the truth is that young Degutis made it possible to fly our nation's flag at a time when such action was considered treason by the Soviets. He went on to help more than 30 Lithuanian dissidents escape to freedom. It is because men like him did not survive that we must make every effort to remember them."

Interest in Lithuanian history has been on the rise recently, with the success of the award-winning memoir, *Love Songs of the Revolution*. The book was written under a pseudonym and the true identity of the author is not known. In the book, Degutis helps the author escape to safety but is killed by a fellow freedom fighter. Degutis disappeared in 1989 and his body was never found.

The iron wolf statue will be situated on the terrace in the middle level of the garden, near a set of pillars modeled after the three pillars of Gediminas. It will accompany the first sculpture placed in the Lithuanian Cultural Garden in 1936, a bust of Dr. Jonas Basanavičius, a scholar, historian, and first president of the Lithuanian Republic.

The Lithuanian garden is one of 26 gardens that make up the Cleveland Cultural Gardens, located within Rockefeller Park. Other gardens in the park include the Polish, Armenian, African-American and Chinese Gardens. Combined, these gardens reveal the history of immigration to the United States. They comment on how we have built communities and constructed our identities as individuals and collectives.

Lithuanian-American artist Nancy Shimkus was commissioned to create the iron wolf statue.

The unveiling ceremony will begin at 10 a.m. The Cleveland Cultural Gardens are located at 690 E. 88th St. The Lithuanian garden is number 12 on the map, between the Greek and German gardens.

###

EXTRA NO. 11

Pages from the Atwater Social Endowment Fund's tax returns for 2009

(redacted)

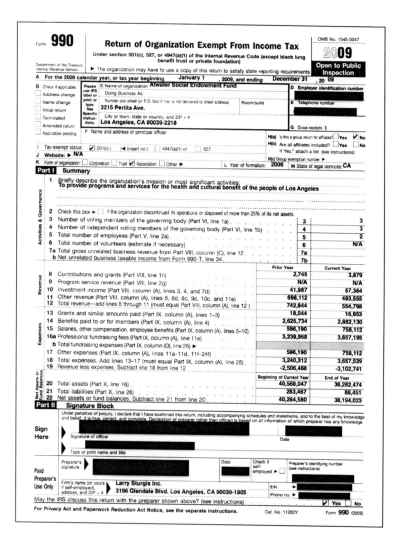

Form 990 (2009)

Page **7**

Part VII Compensation of Officers, Directors, Trustees, Key Employees, Highest Compensated Employees, and Independent Contractors

Section A. Officers, Directors, Trustees, Key Employees, and Highest Compensated Employees

1a Complete this table for all persons required to be listed. Report compensation for the calendar year ending with or within the organization's tax year. Use Schedule J-2 if additional space is needed.

- List all of the organization's **current** officers, directors, trustees (whether individuals or organizations), regardless of amount of compensation. Enter -0- in columns (D), (E), and (F) if no compensation was paid.
- List all of the organization's **current** key employees. See instructions for definition of "key employee."
- List the organization's five **current** highest compensated employees (other than an officer, director, trustee, or key employee) who received reportable compensation (Box 5 of Form W-2 and/or Box 7 of Form 1099-MISC) of more than $100,000 from the organization and any related organizations.
- List all of the organization's **former** officers, key employees, and highest compensated employees who received more than $100,000 of reportable compensation from the organization and any related organizations.
- List all of the organization's **former directors or trustees** that received, in the capacity as a former director or trustee of the organization, more than $10,000 of reportable compensation from the organization and any related organizations.

List persons in the following order: individual trustees or directors; institutional trustees; officers; key employees; highest compensated employees; and former such persons.

☐ Check this box if the organization did not compensate any current officer, director, or trustee.

(A) Name and Title	(B) Average hours per week	(C) Position (check all that apply)						(D) Reportable compensation from the organization (W-2/1099-MISC)	(E) Reportable compensation from related organizations (W-2/1099-MISC)	(F) Estimated amount of other compensation from the organization and related organizations
		Individual trustee or director	Institutional trustee	Officer	Key employee	Highest compensated employee	Former			
Antanas Kudirka Chairman and Executive Director	10	✔				✔		2,248,061	0	0
Prescott Adams Trustee		✔						0	0	0
Agné Mielkuté Vice-Chairman				✔				0	0	0
Larry Sturgis Treasurer				✔				0	0	0
Vincent Neris Secretary				✔				0	0	0
Pierre Kudirka Director of Programs	15					✔		634,068	0	0

LENGTH: 3813 words
HEADLINE: Gintaras Degutis discusses *Love Songs of the Revolution*
ANCHORS: TERRY GROSS
BODY:

TERRY GROSS, host:
This is **FRESH AIR**. I'm Terry Gross.

Three years ago, a memoir called *Love Songs of the Revolution* won the National Book Critics Circle Award for autobiography. The author was a Lithuanian painter named Martynas Kudirka, and his book told the story of his search for his wife's killer. She was murdered during the revolutionary upheaval that ultimately ended Soviet control of the Baltic states of Lithuania, Latvia and Estonia.

In the book, Martynas comes home one day in 1989 to find his wife, Dr. Natalie Milosz, dead on the kitchen floor with a knife in her back. When Martynas realizes the police aren't interested in finding his wife's murderer, he sets out to find the killer himself. Martynas's amateur investigation into Natalie's death turns out to be a voyage of discovery. Natalie was not the faithful wife and stalwart Communist party member he'd thought her to be.

For one thing, he discovers that Natalie had been having an affair with another scientist, a woman named Dr. Indre Bučienė. Even more surprising, he learns that his wife had been heavily involved with Lithuania's underground pro-independence movement. She had been collecting papers documenting crimes by members of the Soviet Lithuanian government, from the current day to as far back as World War II.

In the end, Martynas and his wife's lover, Indre, decide to finish the work Natalie had been involved in, at great risk to themselves. They deliver a package of sensitive documents to a group of independence activists. But when they do, Indre is killed on the streets during a demonstration, and Martynas is forced to flee the country. One of his wife's students, another independence activist named Gintaras Degutis, helps Kudirka escape to safety. But in the book, even as they arrive safely in Sweden, Gintaras is killed accidentally by a fellow independence activist who actually wants Martynas killed because he doesn't trust him. The man who killed Natalie and Indre turns out to be a thug named Pablo, working for the burgeoning Russian mafia. If you can follow all that. It's a complicated story of shifting alliances in the Soviet era Eastern bloc.

That is the end of the book, but it's not the end of the story. Shortly after the book was published, what was a thriller became a whodunit. Almost as soon as *Love Songs of the Revolution* won the prize and became a bestseller, questions about the author's identity and his story began to spring up. There were also questions of fact. For example, in the book, a man who appears to be a CIA agent is killed, but the CIA has stated publically none of their agents were killed in Lithuania at that time. Later, a graduate student of Lithuanian descent who questioned the role of these secret documents in overthrowing the government traveled to Vilnius to conduct research on the book and try to find the author. She ended up dead in what police are saying was murder. Her killer has not been found.

Two weeks ago a Lithuanian-American man named Gintaras Degutis came forward, announcing he is, in fact, the author of *Love Songs of the Revolution*. Yes, that's the same name as Natalie's young student, who helped her husband flee the country and gets killed at the end of the book. Here to help us sort fact from fiction is Gintaras Degutis. Gintaras, welcome to Fresh Air.

Mr. GINTARAS DEGUTIS: Thank you, Terry.

GROSS: Gintaras, I've just told the story, the narrative as it appears in the book. Why don't you begin by telling the story that has emerged since it was published?

Mr. DEGUTIS: When the book first appeared, it did exactly what I expected. There wasn't much of an audience for it in the general American population, but it was very popular within the Lithuanian community here in the U.S. Then it was announced as a finalist for the National Book Critics Circle award, and many unexpected things happened very quickly. Sales went through the roof, and people started picking apart details. The CIA statement. Martynas, Natalie and Indre aren't real people. And so on. When that poor student, Delaney Cantor, put together the name of Antanas Kudirka and discovered him to be a former KGB agent, a whole new story began. I am told that police in Vilnius believe the woman who contacted Ms. Cantor for the meeting she talks about on the Twitter, lured her to her death.

GROSS: Really?

Mr. DEGUTIS: Yes, but they have not been able to find this woman. I believe she was in fact working for Antanas Kudirka.

GROSS: But in the pictures we've seen of Antanas Kudirka, he's a wizened, eighty-something year old man.

Mr. DEGUTIS: That is how he would like you to see him. In truth, Antanas Kudirka has run the American branch of Lithuania's largest mafia for many years, from his home in Los Angeles. His name and face are now in the public eye, something he has fought to prevent ever since he left Lithuania. When Ms. Cantor named him, she put herself in terrible danger.

GROSS: How do you know so much about Antanas Kudirka?

Mr. DEGUTIS: He once tried to kill me, just as I wrote in the ending of the book. I also know of many other men and women he killed in Lithuania. I was there when he killed Kurt Parable, an innocent man who had gone to Lithuania in search of his father. I am certain Antanas killed the people that I call Natalie Milosz and Indre Bučienė in the book.

GROSS: Why? Who was he working for?

Mr. DEGUTIS: Antanas Kudirka was a hired thug in those days, working for the highest bidder. For years it was the

Party and the KGB. He killed so many, many people. When capitalism became the law of the land, he worked for the people with money and power. Very often, it was the same people from before, only they had much more money to pay him. He worked his way up the ranks in the mafia, and when he came to America, he continued his work. Every Lithuanian living in America knows about his organized crime syndicate, but no one speaks up about it because either they have benefitted from the syndicate and its charities, or because they are terrified of him.

GROSS: You accuse him of quite a lot.

Mr. DEGUTIS: You have to understand, Antanas Kudirka is an evil man. An evil product of his environments, I should say. When the communists paid him, he believed in their rhetoric and sang the *Internationale*. When the capitalists came along, he became one of them and took their money. Each in its extreme generates its own kind of evil, and the difference between the two is less than you might imagine.

GROSS: What do you mean?

Mr. DEGUTIS: Perhaps the differences seem smaller for those of us who have lived under both systems. In the Soviet era, it was the state who told us how we could and could not live. Here in America, it is the corporations that control our lives, and we are willing participants. Corporations decide what we will see on television and in the movies, what will appear in newspapers, what chemicals and inedible ingredients will be put into our food. If a government did those things to them, Americans would protest, but because

174

something called a corporation does it to them, they pay money for it and beg for more.

GROSS: But evil is a strong word.

Mr. DEGUTIS: This can be difficult to explain to Americans, because your sense of the word "evil" is limited by theater and politicking, which in this country often amount to the same thing. So when you hear the word "evil," you might think "Evil Empire" or "Axis of Evil." You imagine some kind of James Bond nemesis rubbing his hands together and plotting to take over the world. As Lithuanians, we grew up knowing a kind of evil that is more mundane and many times more terrifying because it is so real. For centuries we have lived in the shadow of powers that have sought to drive us off our land, destroy our language and culture, and make us slaves. If not genocide by the Nazis, then genocide by the Soviets. Or by their Tsarist forebears.

GROSS: A self-published memoir by a retired colonel claims Kurt was the son of a Lockheed engineer who went over to the Soviet side, and you now claim you were there when he was killed.

Mr. DEGUTIS: I believe the colonel's story to be by and large true. In July of 1989, Kurt Parable showed up in Lithuania and contacted someone in the independence movement. I was assigned to help him find his father. My professor, the woman I call Natalie, used her connections in the scientific community to confirm that a man known in Lithuania as Robertas Parabolas had been on the U-2 and had in fact survived the crash. When Kurt came to our country, Robertas was living with a Lithuanian wife and children in a small town. I took Kurt there to look for him. Antanas must have followed us all the way from Vilnius. We were walking through a quiet residential neighborhood when Antanas grabbed Kurt, dragged him into an empty apartment and killed him. He used his favorite method, a knife.

GROSS: But you survived.

Mr. DEGUTIS: I ran. I had to. It was not my finest hour. I ran to save my own life, but I also ran because Kurt was an American. As a member of the independence movement I couldn't be caught anywhere near his dead body. It would have put many other people in danger.

GROSS: Do you think it is true that Kurt's father, Robert Parable, worked for the Soviets?

Mr. DEGUTIS: Yes. Natalie had all the details. The day after the crash Robertas Parabolas was found wandering through the Lithuanian countryside trying to buy off peasants with gold Napoleons. The Soviets contacted the US government quietly, through diplomatic back channels. The Americans at first denied the flight even happened, just like with the more famous Francis Gary Powers crash, which happened very soon after that. When the Americans realized the Soviets had the plane, they insisted it was a weather mission for NASA. When they discovered that Parabolas had been on the plane and survived, they shut down communications entirely. By then, the Powers U-2 had gone down inside Russian territory, and that was all the Russians or the Americans cared about. The Americans were not interested in negotiating for Parabolas. The story in Lithuania was that Parabolas became embittered by this treatment by his own people, and decided to work for the Soviets.

GROSS: Do you really think the Americans refused to negotiate for the release of one of the best aerospace engineers in the country? That's a lot to swallow.

Mr. DEGUTIS: I don't have evidence to prove or disprove it. Robertas Parabolas believed it and acted accordingly. He settled down with a young woman he had met while wandering the countryside after the crash. He made a life for himself in Lithuania. He continued his work in his newfound home. When the son he had left back in America came looking for him, the KGB sent Antanas Kudirka to kill the younger Parabolas.

GROSS: You now say he also killed Natalie Milosz, although in the book a man named Pablo killed her. The way I'm reading it, Pablo is Antanas. Correct?

Mr. DEGUTIS: The man I call "Pablo" in the book did most of the things that Antanas did in real life.

GROSS: But in the book, when the narrator Martynas Kudirka finds his wife's body, she is clutching a paper written by you. Why did you put yourself under suspicion?

Mr. DEGUTIS: I found Natalie's body. That is the truth. It is true she was a professor and that she was active in the independence movement, as was I. One day I went to her apartment with information she was expecting, and found here there sprawled on the kitchen floor, a pool of blood beneath her. In truth, Natalie's hands were empty when I found her.

In my first draft of the book, the character of Natalie was in love with me and on the verge of leaving Martynas. But that was fantasy, and it was not fair to Natalie's memory. So the only false connection I created in the book was to put that paper in her hands. I wanted some part of me to be with her forever. Yes, I was in love with her, but she loved another woman in the movement. Kudirka killed both of those beautiful women, and it broke my heart.

GROSS: Are you Martynas Kudirka?

Mr. DEGUTIS: No! There never was a Martynas Kudirka. Or if there was, he was not a killer. Nor did he write a book about trying to solve his wife's murder.

GROSS: Then why did you make up this man when you wrote this book?

Mr. DEGUTIS: To protect myself. When I fled to the U.S. in 1989, I was certain I would never return to Lithuania. I had helped so many others escape to safety that I was known to the KGB, and I was in very real danger. Although I felt sure Lithuania was on the cusp of change—and thank God it turned out we were right about that—I also knew that the end of the Soviet Union was not the end of danger. When I fled from the Port of Klaipeda on that rusty barge, I was trying to save only one person: myself. When I arrived at the Port of Visby on Gotland, Swedish territory, Antanas was waiting for me with a gun. I survived the shooting, but I knew that if he would shoot me in the West, there was nowhere safe for me to go. When I wrote the book, even though so many years had passed, I knew it was still very dangerous. I had to disguise myself. I tried to, anyway.

GROSS: Why did you write it? If you were so afraid for your safety, the safest thing would have been not to write the book at all.

Mr. DEGUTIS: I had to write the book. You see, when I came to America, I decided to settle into a quiet life in a small city where I could be ordinary. No more politics, no more danger. I eventually came to work in an office where I spent my days pushing papers about and quietly eating my soup. But even as I tried to forget my beloved city and my dissident years, the memory of what Antanas Kudirka had done to Natalie burned inside me. When that horrible man reappeared in my life, I could not let him go to his grave without facing justice.

GROSS: How did he reappear?

Mr. DEGUTIS: It was fate, something so improbable that it could not be an accident. The company where I work subcontracts to a subcontractor to the IRS. My job is to process a very specific IRS form, moving it along an assembly line. I review the lines in the form, then pass it along to the next person. [laughs] My daily routine in the office would make Gogol proud. The only difference between my work and the Soviet bureaucracy is that in America, private companies do the work. At least in the

Soviet Union people who did this kind of work had the hope of a government pension in their old age. In America, you offer even less.

GROSS: So you found Antanas Kudirka through his taxes.

Mr. DEGUTIS: It was the IRS paperwork filed by a charity he has created called the Atwater Social Endowment Fund. One look at the form and you'll see he's using this so-called charity to launder money, paying himself and someone named Pierre Kudirka ridiculously high salaries. When I saw the name, I simply had to find out if it was the same Antanas Kudirka I had known, so I started digging. When I connected him to the Lithuanian mafia, an organization everyone in our community knows and fears, part of me wished I had never gone digging. The other part of me was enraged. This evil man was living a full life surrounded by family and riches— this Pierre is his son. It wasn't right. I had to do something about it.

GROSS: And your solution was to write a memoir that doesn't include his name, and in fact includes a lot of incidents and people that turn out to be entirely false.

Mr. DEGUTIS: "False" is an unfair word here. At its essence, what *Love Songs of the Revolution* reveals is historical truths. That was my intent. I could not write a book that simply told the facts in chronological order with actual names. That would get me killed. Instead, I wrote a book with enough clues to lead a good researcher to the facts. My mistake was that I assumed American readers and researchers would be interested in the story and the text. Instead they turned out to be far more interested in the author. Rather than track down the story, they tried to track down me. I suppose this is a sign I don't really understand my adopted country. Looking back, I realize I should have expected this in America, home to a most venerable cult of the personality. I don't understand why the author matters at all. I wrote a story and I wanted it to be read.

GROSS: Well, many people would say that the author matters because this story was sold to readers as a memoir, and the credibility of a memoir rests on the credibility of its author. I mean, can we even be sure you really are the author of this book?

Mr. DEGUTIS: A fair question, Terry. An investigative reporter from the New York Times came to me and asked the same question. He has taken files from my computer for some kind of forensic testing. He has all the files, including early drafts and scenes I later deleted from the final book. Those files date back to well before the publication date. His research will prove that I am the author.

GROSS: What about all the factual errors in the book? Certain cafes and shops, the timing of the shortages. Some Lithuanians have said it couldn't have been written by anyone who lived in Cold War Vilnius. Has it been so long ago that you forgot what Vilnius was like?

Mr. DEGUTIS: Don't you see, Terry? That was the point. I was true to the Vilnius that I loved, and true to the hidden truths of our lives. These so-called errors that readers have discovered were intentional. They were part of the trail of clues I left for readers to follow. They were intended to raise questions, and lead you to the truth underlying the book.

GROSS: At the end of the book you decided to kill yourself off. Why? When you wrote this book, did you think of yourself as dead?

Mr. DEGUTIS: Not at all. I killed myself to protect myself, and it was a difficult decision. My editor first suggested that I write a happy ending, where Martynas and I get away safely and Antanas is killed. As much as I hated it, I wrote that ending. When my editor read it, both of us agreed it was very stupid. Which was good, because by then I had decided that I needed to be dead by the end of the book. If I used my real name and ended up dead, I thought anyone who recognized me or cared enough to do any research would assume I was in fact dead. I wanted Antanas Kudirka to believe that he did kill me when he shot me on Gotland in 1989.

GROSS: When you wrote the book you wanted people to believe you were dead. Now you do want to be known. Why have you changed your mind?

Mr. DEGUTIS: When I wrote the book, I thought the best way to keep myself safe was to stay hidden. Now that the book has captured so much attention, I believe the best way to keep myself safe is to be as visible as I possibly can.

GROSS: At the beginning of the book, you wrote that, "The story I am going to tell is true; therefore it will not please you." Now, while *Love Songs* is a pleasure to read, it's the story since the book was published that I have to tell you, quite frankly, has me completely confused. Every time I think I've sorted out one true fact from your story, I find out something else about your life or that time period that doesn't fit.

Mr. DEGUTIS: You are trying to make sense of that which cannot make sense, Terry. In our lives today, we are constantly pelted with disconnected bits and bytes of information that don't add up to anything at all. We as humans constantly try to construct some kind of grand narrative that will make sense of the world and of our lives. But that grand narrative we construct is inevitably less true than the sum of its parts.

This is the source of so much popular Cold War nostalgia on both sides of the Iron Curtain today. People look back on that era and remember it as a happier, simpler time when each side had its own grand narrative—communism or capitalism. The global struggle between those two behemoths served as an even grander meta-narrative that gave meaning to our meaningless lives.

But in our nostalgia, we forget how all of us lived in mortal terror that any day, at any moment, we could blow each other off the face of the Earth with our ridiculous weapons of mass destruction. On the Soviet side, they trained us to have the pride to die for our ideology. On your side, you were trained to shop and play and live life as if there were no tomorrow. All of us were terrorized on a scale both epic and personal. Still, somehow, our collective fear of dying in a thermonuclear war was less true than our individual fears of ending up like Natalie and Indre. The war never came, but those two beautiful women died, which was a tragedy. We believed in false grand narratives that hid the deeper truths of our individual lives. This is the truth of my book.

GROSS: Gintaras Degutis, thank you so much for talking with us.

ACKNOWLEDGEMENTS

Many thanks to literary impresario Jason Pettus and his team at the Chicago Center for Literature and Photography (CCLaP), especially my editor Sarah Bradford. Thanks also to Lori Baker-Schena, my publicist and cheerleader-in-chief. Tough critiques from the Tuesday night group at Writers at Work helped make this book better—my thanks to each of you. To Terry Wolverton, I'm grateful for your years of support as friend and mentor. Melissa Wall, thank you for taking me places I might never have gone.

BRONWYN MAULDIN, creator of *GuerrillaReads*, the online video literary magazine, won *The Coffin Factory* magazine's 2012 very short story award for *Měiguó*, her story exploring the unexpected dangers of international migration. Her previous work includes the short story collection, **The Streetwise Cycle**, and a Kindle single, **Body of Work**. Mauldin's work, which spans both fiction and nonfiction, has appeared in *CellStories*, *The Battered Suitcase*, *Blithe House Quarterly*, *Clamor* magazine and *From ACT-UP to the WTO*. She is a host of *Indymedia on Air* on KPFK, the Los Angeles affiliate of the Pacifica radio network, and is a researcher with the Los Angeles County Arts Commission.

CPSIA information can be obtained
at www.ICGtesting.com
Printed in the USA
FFOW03n0127210814
6964FF